SARAYAH DANIELLE

What We Consume

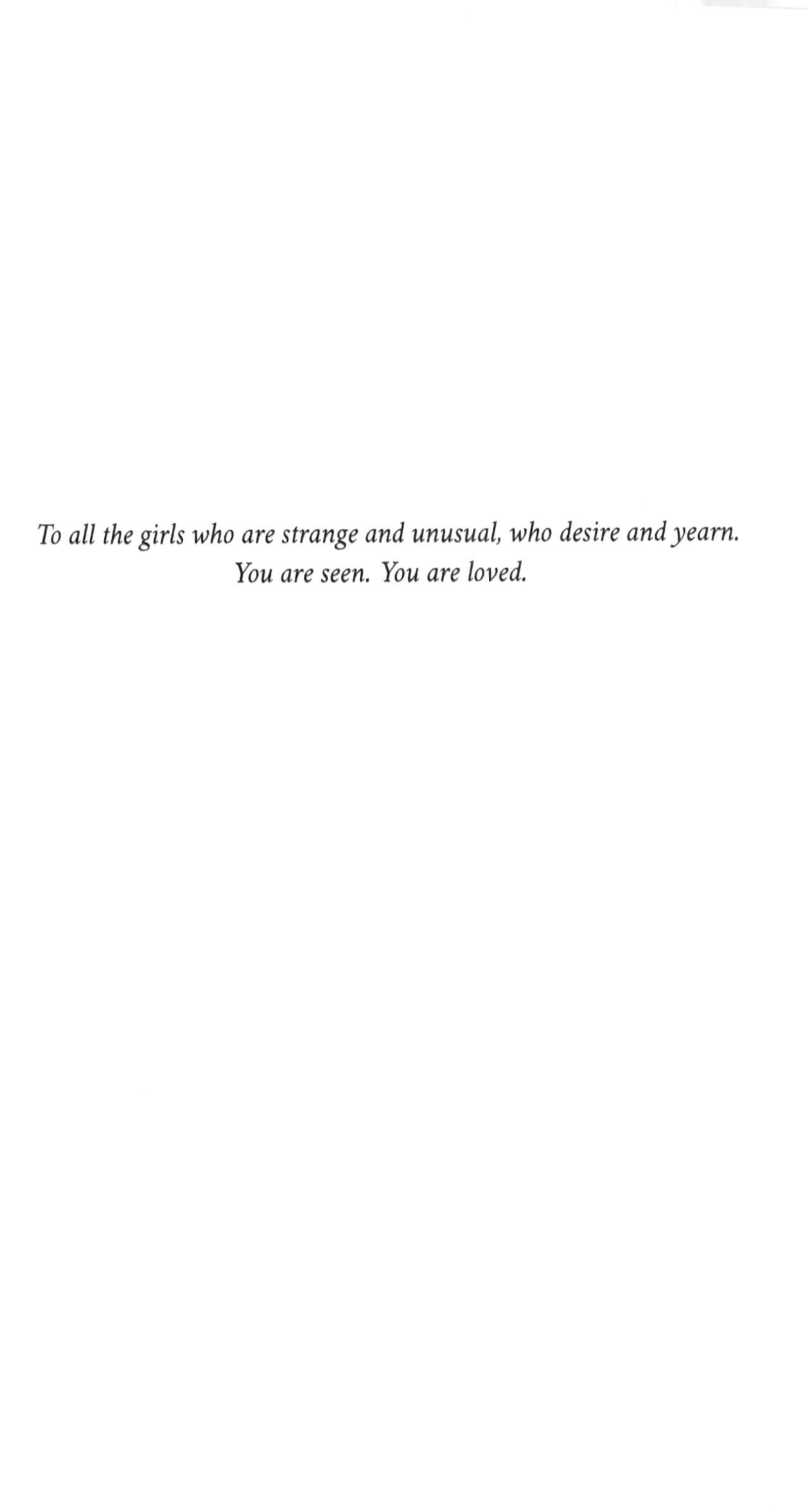

To all the girls who are strange and unusual, who desire and yearn.
You are seen. You are loved.

"Come away, O human child!
To the waters and the wild
With a faery, hand in hand,
For the world's more full of weeping
than you can understand."

— W.B. Yeats

Contents

Aislin - Present	1
Aislin - Middle School	12
Aislin - Present	29
Breena - Present	46
Breena - Middle School	63
Breena - Present	83
Vivien - Present	94
Vivien - Middle School	107
Vivien - Present	122
Acknowledgments	140
Sneak Peak: "Promises to Keep"	142
About the Author	154

Aislin - Present

Depending on where you started the story, it started with Aislin O'Malley. She drove deep into the woods, down the long winding roads leading to the Freel family cabin. Her cell reception had dropped about half an hour ago, but she had memorized the route by heart. She'd know the way even with her eyes closed, as if the twists and curves of the route had been carved into the backs of her eyelids.

There had been a storm the night before, but the day had steadily grown warmer, and the air smelt of rain-soaked dirt and sun-dried leaves. Aislin loved this time of year, when spring teetered into summer like a toddler learning to walk, never sure if it could fully commit to the transition. The sun had already dipped towards the horizon, painting the forest in a swath of bruise purples and yellows. She had left later than she had originally wanted to, but that was to be expected. It was her first time in a long while driving up to the cabin with another passenger after all.

When she and the girls were in high school, they would all get up at the break of dawn and pile into Poppy's parent's van and drive up to the cabin. Breena and Vivien would blast Evanescence and Nirvana through the car stereo, while Poppy drove, and Aislin dealt out the snacks. They'd do anything just to get away from Devil's Pointe, even going as far as to tell Poppy's parents that they were using the cabin for Bible study. The Freels never cared much for what Poppy, or the rest of the girls got up to, as long as it didn't get back to the congregation and embarrass them. Almost every teenager in Devil's Pointe was doing drugs or partying or sleeping with some sleazy person they met at the gas station just off Route 5, so it was easy for the girls to fly under the radar.

No one liked spilling secrets when they could get their own misdeeds brought to light. Everyone watched everyone. As much as they all wanted to pretend, secrets didn't really exist in Devil's Pointe.

Now it had become something of a ritual for the remaining three to make the trip just before dusk so they could soak up the last rays of the sun in solitude. Aislin had the windows rolled down so she could feel the wind brushing through her hair like the tips of Poppy's fingers while the radio static played in the background—the station she liked always cut out about 15 minutes into the trip.

Even with Poppy gone, the Freels still let the girls use their cabin whenever they needed to get away, which surprised Aislin. They wanted to sell it after everything had happened, but no one would buy it. It sat on the market for a year before the Freels decided that it would be less work to just keep it. They let the girls do whatever they wanted with the cabin and in return, never had to deal with it again.

Had Breena and Vivien made it up yet? Vivien was always the first one to make it up and she'd usually be cooking or sitting in front of a roaring fire with a book in her lap by the time Aislin arrived. Breena was almost always last. She was perpetually late to everything. *Time is made up*, she always said with a wave of her hand or a heavy sigh as she settled onto the carpet at Vivien's feet.

"Do you want me to change the radio station?" Jamie asked. She had gotten pretty good at pretending he wasn't there. But alas, there he was, sat in the passenger seat fiddling with his camera, not bothering to even look over at her as he spoke. Aislin supposed she couldn't blame him. He wasn't interested in her or anything she had to say while the camera was off. He didn't want to risk missing out on any vital material, so Aislin kept mostly quiet throughout their trip, aside from basic questions and answers.

"I'd like to keep it if you don't mind. I kind of like it." She shook her head and turned the radio's volume up a bit, "It's like white noise. You won't find any other stations this far into the mountains."

"Where exactly are we?"

"We're in the White Mountains, just a few hours outside Devil's Pointe."

Jamie hummed in acknowledgment as he adjusted his camera, peering through the viewfinder. It looked like he was getting shots of the trees surrounding them, likely to add to the dramatics of his documentary. Aislin didn't know much about Jamie, aside from the basics she could find on his blog and social media. He had reached out to Vivien, and she had relayed everything back to Aislin and Breena.

Aislin hadn't been too keen about the documentary, but she didn't mind too much. Having Jamie in the cabin with them would be weird, but they had dealt with worse. Breena had been vehemently against it. She and Vivien spent three days arguing about it, until Breena finally acquiesced. The idea of letting him into their yearly drive up to their cabin, their ritual, their mourning. It felt like a cat playing with the mouse invading its home before killing it.

He was a complete stranger, and it felt odd for him to be filming something so private.

We're so solitary. I think it might be good for us to talk about it all. Vivien could convince them to do anything with a mere bat of her lashes and a coy smile. It was hard to say no to her.

All she really knew about Jamie was that he was a young filmmaker that had just graduated from NYU, and he had won some kind of major indie film award for this overly macabre movie he made his freshman year. It had been some horror flick about a little girl that got stolen away by the faeries. Vivien had found it enjoyable, but Aislin could barely stomach the first few scenes. Breena didn't even bother watching the film.

From what Vivien told her, his movies were hailed as gospel within a few niche online film groups, and though he typically gravitated towards horror, he wanted to try dipping his toes into the world of true crime documentaries.

What better way to jump into the water than with the Lambs?

It's what the media decided to call them after they had been found. The Lambs—something to do with the sacrificial way the girls had been posed in the woods and the gauzy white dresses they were wearing when the police finally found them. She still had the dress—held onto it out of some morbid desire to be close to Poppy. Vivien and Breena still had theirs too.

Aislin shook the thoughts of that night away. She didn't like looking at it too closely. Didn't like the way it made her stomach stir or heat rise to her face.

Jamie didn't look like any of the other fans Aislin had met before, she didn't even know if he was a fan. He must have been if he was willing to spend an entire weekend filming and interviewing them, but he also could have just been desperate, not wanting to lose the fame he had come into so quickly.

"So, now that I've got the camera all set up," Jamie spun the camera to face her, "Why don't you start?"

"Oh, I don't—I mean this whole thing is a little weird for me. I'm sure you know but we don't usually do interviews, like ever. I don't even go to my own art auctions. I wouldn't even know where to start." After all the police interrogations and the media frenzy that surrounded them in the months following the incident, the girls had made a pact promising one another to stay out of the spotlight. They didn't want the attention, the *fame*. Nothing good came out of what happened, and they didn't want to act like something had.

"Why do you all hide in the shadows? You guys are famous. Most people wouldn't look that gift horse in the mouth." Jamie chuckled under his breath.

Aislin's hands tightened on the steering wheel until her knuckles turned white. "I guess, we don't want to be a spectacle. It's not right to gain fame for what happened. It would feel dishonorable to her memory."

"Her as in Poppy."

Aislin nodded, rubbing the tips of her fingers together to ease the tension in her body.

"Tell me about her. She's where it all kind of started right?"

And there was the command: *Tell me about Poppy.*

Tell me about Poppy. Tell me what it was like to be friends with Poppy. Did you hate her? Do you miss her? Did you love her too much? Did she make you feel inferior? Did you hate her? Why didn't she come back? Why did you come back?

"What do you want to know?" Aislin asked. There was so much Aislin could say, even more that she wouldn't.

"Start at the beginning. How'd you all become friends?"

Aislin stiffened at the question. It wasn't the line of questioning she was used to. There didn't seem to be an ulterior motive behind his words. *How'd you all become friends?* It felt…innocent. So innocent she wanted to burst out laughing. She nearly did, and she had to bite her tongue so hard to stop herself that she almost bled.

She rolled her answer around in her mouth for a moment. With the sun almost gone and the moon rising higher in the sky by the minute, the air was getting cooler, causing goosebumps to rise across Jamie's skin. The cold never quite reached Aislin. She was always cold, so it rarely bothered her.

"Well, I guess I was technically the first out of our group to meet Poppy. Our parents grew up in the church together, so once my dad moved us back to town, Poppy and I were always around one another. We didn't talk much, just spent most of our lives staring at one another from across the dinner table or sharing a pew during service. But we didn't really become friends until we met Breena and Vivien when we were thirteen. *The scariest age for girls*, my stepmother used to say. When you're right on the precipice of childhood, standing on that cliff ready to jump into the golden age of being a teen. I guess we were these bored, fragile little creatures so we tied ourselves to the closest thing we could find."

"And what was that?" Jamie asked.

Aislin scoffed; the answer was obvious. "Poppy. She was like our planet, and we were the moons orbiting around her."

"That sounds intense."

Intense was an understatement. Most of their teen-hood was spent worshiping Poppy like a deity. With her, they were grounded: given an ideal to match, an orbit to follow. They always knew where they were going when the four of them were together. What they didn't realize at the time was that Poppy worshiped them just the same.

Aislin let out a nervous chuckle, "Being tied to each other like we all were—it was like being in a fairy tale and your worst nightmare all at the same time. Where one went, the rest followed. No matter what. And when we tried pulling away from one another, it was like we were ripping at the seams that held us together. We were teenagers. We lived our lives in absolutes. All black. All white. Never an in-between."

"What was so special about Poppy?" His question was too flippant, too casual. *What was so special about Poppy?*

Everything. There was nothing ordinary about her.

"She just had a knack for showing up when you needed her. Even when you didn't know it yourself. When my dad died, suddenly she was everywhere: sitting with me at lunch, walking me to school, singing with me at church."

"You have stepsisters. Were you not close to them?"

What could she really say about her sisters? That she had wanted to hack at their hair while they were sleeping? Burn their favorite dresses and gifts that their mother, Mavis, had given them? Paint their lockers with pig's blood or put dead animals in their beds like they had done to her so many times?

"We weren't really close, but I didn't hate them. They had only been married into the family for a short while before my dad died, so we didn't have a lot of time to bond. It felt like I was the only one really grieving him, so I suppose a part of me resented them for that." She picked at a hangnail on her thumb and when it started to bleed, she brought it to her mouth, savoring the way it coated her tongue.

There was a hidden path just off to the right of the road

that led to her father's old cabin. When her father was still around, the two of them would drive up to this neck of the woods every Christmas and spend the week making snowmen, drinking hot chocolate, and telling scary stories. Her dad had been a writer, not a very prolific one or a very famous one, but everyone in Devil's Pointe had owned a copy of at least one of his novels. Aislin had always loved his stories—dark tales of young maidens being stolen away in the woods or children being snatched from their cradles when their parents' backs were turned away.

Aislin had learned at a young age that the woods were nothing but trouble. She had spent most of her childhood half terrified of the forests that sat at the edge of Devil's Pointe. Her father had always warned her to keep her wits about her. *The trees keep secrets. They aren't your friends.*

What her father hadn't known was that there were far worse things hidden in the forest than the trees.

"Poppy made me feel seen. Like my pain was real. Like it mattered."

Jamie was silent for a moment, but he kept the camera trained on her. Her eyes stayed on the road, but she could feel how he watched her through the lens. Ever since he got in her car, he avoided looking directly at her as if the real thing might taint the image he was putting on film.

"Does anyone feel seen?" He asked.

Aislin shrugged. "No. No one feels seen. That's the burden of being a teenage girl. It's why you spend your years searching for people who see you and see through you. Searching for people that won't judge you, who will love you unconditionally. No matter how horrible of a person you may be."

The girls just got lucky that they found someone like that so quickly.

"Did you feel like a horrible person?"

Aislin shook her head, her hands tightening on the steering wheel. She couldn't get the word "No" past her lips. It was a lie, or at least it felt like it was. If she explained it to him, would he understand? Would he believe her?

It was dark now, with only the moon and her car's headlights to illuminate the road.

There was an ear-splitting thud as the car jolted over something lying in the road. Aislin could feel the undercarriage of the car scraping against whatever she ran over, and she slammed her foot on the brake, the car screeching to a halt. Jamie swore under his breath as Aislin stared out the windshield, her heart jack-hammering in her chest. She couldn't have hit a person, no one ever just walked this close to the road.

She unbuckled her seatbelt and scrambled out of the car, Jamie following behind. The night was quiet, save for the low rumble of her car's engine and the dinging of her dashboard telling her that the door was open. Her front bumper was dented and there were dark flecks of blood and hair stuck in the grill.

"What the hell did you hit?" Jamie asked, pointing his camera at the front of her car.

Aislin just stared at her car, eyes wide in bewilderment as she took in the clumps of hair caught in her grill and the splatters of blood garnishing her hood. Her stomach knotted at the sight of the blood, anticipation flooding her body. She walked around to the back of her car, wrapping her arms around her middle. The wind bristled through the trees above them, carrying whispered voices that brushed across Aislin's skin. She shivered.

She could feel something watching her from the tree line, but she refused to look up. *Nothing good comes from searching in the shadows.*

Laying in the middle of the road was a doe, sitting in a puddle of blood. Its bright brown fur was now matted and covered in blood so dark it looked almost black. But she hadn't been the one to kill it. The doe's ribs had been pried open, guts splayed across the road, and its middle was now almost wholly flat from her tires. It was barely a few months old.

"What happened to it? A coyote or mountain lion get to it?" Jamie trained his camera on the deer and Aislin could hear the lens zooming in. She wanted to hit him or hit the camera out of his hand. It was gross and, in that moment, he was no better than any gossip monger in Devil's Point. He wanted a story, even if it came at the expense of someone else, someone—or something—innocent.

"There's a lot of things that could've done this," Aislin said. It wasn't just her father who had been wary of the monsters in the forest. There were so many hungry things hiding in the woods. The deer was just another unlucky animal in the wrong place at the wrong time. But it was still so young. So small. Too small to be torn apart the way it was. She wondered how scared it must have been. How alone it must have felt.

"I'm going to move it off of the road and then we can keep driving. The cabin is only a few miles away." She took a few steps back and walked to the car's back door so she could grab the thick blanket she always kept on the seats.

Jamie dropped his camera and looked at her, his eyes wide with confusion. In the glow of the car headlights, she could finally see the blue of his eyes. He looked at her like she was crazy and pointed to the deer at his feet, "You're going to move it?"

Aislin nodded and bent down to gather what she could of the deer into the blanket, "It's the least I can do after running it over. If I leave it here, it'll never get moved."

"It's just a deer. Some animals will probably come along as soon as we leave and drag it off somewhere to eat it."

Aislin waved him off, brushing her fingers over its soft face. Its mother must be worried sick, anxiously pacing the forest looking for its babe.

"Can you even pick it up?" He asked, eyes wide with disbelief.

The doe looked like it weighed little more than 20 pounds. She had carried heavier.

She cradled the poor thing to her chest and walked a few feet off the road. Its head hung limp over her arm, flopping with each step she took, and she could feel its blood seeping through the blanket and into her shirt, but she paid it no mind. It would have been wrong to leave it lying in the road. She found a spot just past the tree line and laid it down in the dirt. Its round, dark eyes stared up at a sky of nothing. The stars hadn't come out yet.

Aislin - Middle School

islin was no stranger to funerals. The first funeral she attended was her mother's, a somber, lonely affair that passed by in the blink of an eye. So, unlike her father's funeral, which had been packed full of gossiping people with nothing better to do than ruin a family's mourning.

Everyone had been dressed in their fanciest black outfits, including her stepmother and sisters, while she had worn the nicest looking thing she could find stuffed away in the attic. They were moth bitten and a little wrinkled, but they did the job.

The ladies with their freshly curled hair and shiny pearl necklaces and obnoxiously big rings had disagreed. Between taking turns scoffing at Aislin's attire and bad mouthing her parents, they would grab their children by the shoulders and whisper to them some nonsense all while pointing at her and shaking their heads.

It became a game. Someone new would shuffle in, they'd sigh with their hand over their hearts, give a little sniffle, listen to the whispers of the other women, and then came the scoff, their hands on the children's shoulders, the pointing. It happened every fifteen minutes and Aislin had taken to counting out the time between each scoff to keep busy.

She hadn't liked the way they all stared at her, like she was some exotic injured animal, and they didn't know whether she would lick them or bite them. Aislin didn't know which she would do either, but if the whispers continued, she wouldn't know how to be nice.

They talked about her as if she wasn't standing in the same room as them and they loved to speak ill of the dead. Soon all the words had started blending together and she would only catch glimpses of sentences:

How could he...

Wasted potential...

Pathetic excuse of...

But then, Pastor Freel had walked into the room with his wife and all the grating hushed whispers fell and skittered across the floor, like a mouse trying to escape the claws of a cat.

The Freels had made their way to Aislin and her "family," exchanging pleasant smiles that were so forced Aislin could nearly see the strings pulling the Pastor's mouth taut. A rustle of his wife's skirt had dragged Aislin's eyes away from the man. A small, white hand clutched the fabric of the skirt, making it tremble under its grasp. From behind the wife, long auburn hair and wide dark eyes that were too big for their face peered at Aislin.

That was the first time Aislin met Poppy. A moth swirled around in her stomach twisting it up into tiny little knots. When she smiled, Aislin expected to find rows of sharp, pointed, bloodied teeth staring back at her, but she only found the same blunt, little teeth that adorned the inside of Aislin's own mouth.

The girl had said nothing as her eyes roamed over Aislin's messy hair and too big, too wrinkled clothes. But it didn't feel like the judgey gazes of the older women, it felt soft and light.

There was no extra weight behind the girl's stare, there was nothing in it but pure, unadulterated curiosity.

She was just a girl, hiding behind her mother's leg, in a crowd of people sneering down at her.

I see you.

Aislin wanted Poppy to know that she saw her too. Maybe that was why she spent so much time watching her.

They didn't become friends, until much later.

At the start of seventh grade, Aislin and Poppy were put in the same homeroom class. Sometimes while she sat in class, Aislin would peer over her shoulder—eyes innately drawn to Poppy's even from across the room—and watch while Poppy sat at her desk.

That day in March or maybe April she had been gnawing on the end of her pen. She had always had a habit of chewing: her hair, her pencils, her nails. It was like she was perpetually hungry, happy to have anything she could sink her teeth into. Aislin could understand that gnawing feeling that never went away. Sometimes Aislin would stare at Poppy for a bit too long and her teeth would slowly sharpen, her nails would slowly elongate, her eyes would slowly darken. In her mind, Poppy was like a shape-shifter, or a chameleon, either way it had intrigued her.

She had been thankful for the distraction. That morning, she had woken up surrounded by chunks of her own hair. No doubt a surprise from her sisters. Before they had slashed her canvases, ripped apart her drawing notebook, even left a dead mouse in her bed on more than a couple occasions, but they had never *touched* her before. She had cried so hard she vomited into the bathroom sink.

They had always been cruel, but cutting her hair was something beyond them.

She had tried to force herself to refer to them as her stepsisters, but her father had loved them just as much as he loved her before he died, and they had known each other since they were five. They were like almost-sisters. Even if they hated her, they grew up in the same little house, once shared the same little room and the same little toys.

Before her father died, the three of them would share scary stories and play dress up. They'd give each other makeovers and share secrets. Aislin had been so alone for so long that she would have accepted any kind of crumb of attention from Mavis' girls.

A small, strange, rotted part of her still wanted that. Still wanted Mavis' daughters to call her their sister, to let her back into their fold.

Maybe that was why she had always been so enamored with watching Poppy. So enamored that she hadn't even realized that the pen had broken, blackish blue ink spilling down the side of Poppy's small mouth.

Poppy gave her the same feeling that had unfurled in her stomach when she had been introduced to Mavis' girls. It was a spark of connection—a recognition of shared loneliness that they could unburden each other of.

Poppy paused, lithe fingertips dragging across her chin to collect the dark liquid leaking from between her lips. Aislin grabbed a tissue from her pencil case and reached back to place it on Poppy's desk without the teacher noticing. She hadn't waited for a thank you or a smile of gratitude, she simply turned back around and fiddled with the assignment sitting on her desk, scribbling nonsense pictures in the corners.

Aislin didn't care much for school and her stepmother didn't pay much attention to her anyways unless she was getting into trouble or outshining Mavis' *actual* daughters. So, Aislin did what she could to stay invisible. She did well enough to get by in her classes and kept to her room when she was home. She never spoke out of turn, cleaned up after meals. She never invited friends around to the house, not that she had many friends to invite anyways. She didn't join any clubs or after-school activities.

Even still, it hadn't really worked. She still dealt with the long stares from the boys and girls in the hallways before they quickly avoided her eyes, and the whispers began. She couldn't make out everything being said about her, but she always heard little snippets as she passed them. Most were rumors her sisters had spread about her—stupid little girl rumors, wholly outlandish and unbelievable, but nothing was just a rumor in Devil's Pointe. The devil was alive and well in this town and everyone knew there was always a bit of truth in every rumor. They would whisper about how she found mice in the forest and ate them. How she stole locks of her sisters' hair while they were sleeping and used it to curse them.

How ironic. She thought as she ran her fingers over her messy braid that she had put her hair in that morning to hide her own missing chunk of hair. Mavis would have asked questions, and it would have been blamed on Aislin anyways. She knew it would be smart to just cut her hair, so it was all even, but that very thought only made her throat tighten. Her father had always loved her hair. They would spend their nights before bedtime with him brushing it out while she read a story from her book of fairy tales.

She could feel Poppy's eyes follow the movement of Aislin's hand as she tried her best to smooth down the bits of hair that were too short to fully fit into the braid. It was odd, feeling someone watch you. No one really looked at Aislin when she was around. She often felt as if she had become something of a shadow or a ghost to the whole town. But Poppy always saw her, and she always made it obvious, like she was an animal tamer that was slowly approaching a feral beast in the woods, palm outstretched, footfalls gentle and steady.

When the bell rang, Aislin gathered her stuff and walked out of the classroom, Poppy's eyes burning holes into the back of her head. As much as she wanted to talk to Poppy, she needed to get home. It was the last class of the day and Mavis wanted her home so the family could all walk to the church house together for Pastor Freel's special Wednesday service. She didn't know why it was special since it happened every week, but questioning the church never went over well.

There was a small, barely noticeable path Aislin took that cut through the woods behind the school that led directly to her backyard. The path was well-trodden, but Aislin never saw anyone else walking it. The woods were all but desolate in Devil Pointe. Bluebells and foxgloves grew in abundance, and it was as if the trees were frozen in time, forever vibrant and green. It was while walking this path that she could hear the gentle whispers of her father, carried to her on the back of the wind. He told her to stay away, to turn back around, *to run.* But even in death, she wanted to convince him that the forest wasn't all bad. She was still convinced that she could make him change his mind. That she could help him *see* what everyone else couldn't.

To Aislin, the forest was like a soft pair of arms cradling her as she fell asleep—never-changing and constant—but to the rest of the town it was a bad omen. Sure, there was the occasional teen party full of too loud music and underage drinking, or the random misguided lovers' picnic, but most people stayed away. While there were many different stories detailing the horrors of the woods, there was only one that really stuck through the generations.

According to legend, there was a witch who lived in the woods, making potions and casting hexes on the village people who wronged her or treated her unkindly. It was said that she would steal babies from their cribs in the dead of night and replace them with demons or monsters. Her name had been forgotten with time, but Aislin liked to imagine it was something magical like Davina or Willow, possibly Adeline. Unlike the rest of the town, Aislin loved the dark shadows that slithered around her periphery and the hidden animals that snapped twigs underfoot and rustled branches as they silently followed her.

She played with the loose change in the pocket of her cardigan. If her dad were still here, he would never have allowed her to leave the house without a handful of iron shavings in her pocket or a bundle of yarrow. He tried making her a rowan bracelet a few years ago but it made her sick. Since then, she stayed away from rowan just in case it caused another allergic reaction. The yarrow was only slightly better. It didn't make her physically ill like the rowan, but it did leave the pit of her stomach gnarled in little spirals, so she normally kept it deep in her backpack or satchel, as far away from her as possible.

She bent down to gather a bundle of bluebells. Mavis hated when Aislin brought random flowers inside the house, but Aislin had gotten quite good at hiding them beneath her large sweaters or tucking them into her boots. Most of her clothes were too long or too baggy so there was plenty of room to hide things from Mavis and the girls.

Aislin's fingertips brushed up against something wet. Startling back, she peered through the flowers and found a small squirrel quivering in a little puddle of its own blood. She counted each labored rise and fall of its chest as she rubbed her still sticky fingers together. She tamped down her revulsion and wondered what it would feel like if she brought her fingers to her mouth and licked them clean. Would it taste the same as her own blood? Would it be more animal than her own?

Grabbing her sketchbook and pencils, she sat down in the grass. She felt the blades poking at her thighs through her long skirt, pushed her feet into the dirt, and started drawing that now dead animal. It was easier to draw the things that enticed her—Breena's hair, Bethany's shoulders, the dead animal in front of her—than to indulge in them. She kept them locked in the pages of her sketchbook and pushed those thoughts far, far to the back of her mind.

Sometimes she drew the tangled trees, sometimes she drew the sky right before a storm hit, but she always loved to draw flowers, especially the bluebells that abounded in the forests. Her father always warned her away from them. *Those are faerie flowers. If you get too close to them, they'll snatch you away again.*

She thought about him as she drew. He was supposed to be here, lying beside her in the grass or sitting behind her as he braided flowers into her hair. She supposed it was bad of her to miss her father more than her mother. But for most of her life, her father had been a solid substance that would hold her when she had a nightmare or make her blueberry pancakes every Sunday. Her mother had been something intangible—a photo, a dress, a ghost haunting her father's eyes.

She had jumped off the church parapet a few months after Aislin had been born. From the whispers around town, her mother had looked like a swan, flying through the air—white dress billowing around her lithe body, brown hair fluttering behind her round, pale face. Everyone in town called her a paranoid schizophrenic, but her father didn't agree. He always said Aislin's mother was sensitive—sensitive eyes, sensitive ears, sensitive mind. She was delicate, too easy to break. And break she did.

From the pictures in the old photo albums her father kept locked away in his bedside table, Aislin was a mirror image of her mother. They had the same pale, round face. The same mousy brown hair, nearly orange in the right light. But while Aislin's mother had wide blue eyes, Aislin's were nearly black. Too big for her face. *All the better to see the world with.* That's what her father would tell her.

Sometimes, Aislin's father would mistake her for her mother. He had a habit of calling out *Theresa* when he needed something, only to startle, as if from a nightmare, when it was Aislin that walked into the room. Most often, it happened as he were tucking her into bed. In the darkness of her room, he'd kiss her and pet her hair, mumbling *Theresa, Theresa, Theresa.* Afterwards he would fix her nightclothes before softly shutting the door behind him. When he was gone, Aislin would stand by the door and listen to him cry himself to sleep before gathering her blankets and sleeping in her closet.

Sometimes when she thought about it, she imagined what it would feel like to stab him over and over again. She wanted to see him bleed and cry the same way she did.

Aislin pushed those thoughts from her head and focused on

the picture in front of her. It wasn't good to dwell on those memories. She dug her pencil into the paper too hard while shading, tearing through to the next page. Groaning, Aislin tore the page from her notebook and ripped it to shreds.

It was a useless drawing anyway—she couldn't get the shadows right and her lines were too shaky.

The hairs on the back of her neck stood up and Aislin got the distinct feeling she was being watched, like a deer sensing its predator waiting for just the right moment to pounce. But Aislin wasn't a deer.

She waited and listened, but there was only the wind blowing through the trees above her and scattering the loose foliage around the ground. Yet she could feel those eyes trailing her figure. They watched as she finished up her picture and as she put her things back into her bag. The feeling drew closer to her, sending a bolt of lightning up her spine. She spun around, whipping her head towards the eyes watching her. There was something hiding within the shadows, shifting in the darkness. Barely perceptible, but it was there, waiting to strike. She dug her hand into her cardigan pocket and clutched the bundle of yarrow. She was not a deer.

Aislin tossed the bundle into the shadows and ran out of the woods, leaving behind those eyes hiding in the darkness.

When she arrived home, Mavis barely spared her a glance from her spot in the rocking chair by the window.

Her mother's rocking chair. Mavis had never sat in Aislin's mother's rocking chair. At least, until that afternoon.

Rage bubbled in the pit of her stomach at the sight. Not even her father sat in that chair. It had become a sacred object in their home. Too divine to taint with their earthly hands. Aislin wanted to scream at her, to stomp her feet, smash her hands through the stupid picture frames of Mavis and her stupid daughters hanging on the wall.

Don't you understand? That isn't yours. You shouldn't be here. None of this is yours.

Get out.

Get out.

Get out.

But Aislin couldn't say that. Couldn't yell at Mavis. She had only lost her temper once—her first birthday without her father. It didn't matter what she had gotten angry at. By that point, Aislin was angry at everything, but the incident ended with Aislin bent over the ottoman while Mavis whipped her with her belt until the skin of her back split.

So Aislin bit her tongue until she felt the blood wash over her teeth and forced herself to walk up the stairs to get ready for church. She shut the door to her bedroom as quietly as she could, before sitting down on the floor. She stared at the blank, beige wall in front of her trying to slow her racing her heart and focus on anything that wasn't Mavis or her mother or the rocking chair or her father.

Her sisters arrived a few minutes later, stomping their feet around the house as if they needed the very foundation of the home to know they were there. Trying to drown out the noise, Aislin hummed out a song her father used to sing, though she no longer remembered the words. She put on a long beige dress that she kept in the box of her mother's things, hidden away in the attic, and shoved her feet into a pair of scuffed ballet flats, before heading downstairs.

The girls followed Mavis out of the house, Aislin at the very back of the line. Other families milled around the streets, all heading to the church house. Everyone in town went to the Wednesday special services. Except maybe Shannon and Breena Doherty. Aislin watched as they walked hand in hand out of the small pharmacy. Strolling side by side against the current of the town.

Though Shannon Doherty was long rumored to be a witch, it was Breena who received all the harsh glares and mean taunts. She was an easy target, young and impressionable enough to hurt. Aislin sometimes wished that Breena would go to church with the rest of the town, for no other reason than it would be nice to have someone to sit next to. She was so cool with her high-top sneakers and camo pants, graphic t-shirts and flannels that Mavis would never have let Aislin wear. *Girls shouldn't dress like boys.*

The church bell rang out, echoing through the little town square. Shannon grabbed Breena's hand and ushered her back to their home at the very edge of town—so far away it may as well have not been in town at all.

It was only a short walk to the church. Everything in Devil's Pointe was a short walk to the church. The wide doors were open, like the maw of some animal waiting to devour Aislin whole. It lay at the top of a small hill, just at the edge of town. Its once pristine white paint was now beige with age and peeling and the wooden steps creaked under foot, as if they were going to give away at any second. The spring breeze made Aislin's light brown hair flutter around her shoulders as they all walked up. Pastor Freel greeted them all and helped tuck Aislin's hair behind her ears. *It's important to keep your hair out of your face lest you miss God's messages.* He laughed and patted her on the shoulder, steering her inside.

Pastor Freel was always kind, always smiling, always laughing. Aislin didn't like people like that.

Mavis led the girls into the second pew on the right. As Aislin took her seat at the end, the hair on the back of her neck stood up again, just like it did in the forest. She peered up at the row across from her and found Poppy's large dark eyes staring at her. Poppy stayed staring at Aislin as her mother took the seat next to her, smiling up at her husband as he greeted the last few members of the town. A slow smile formed across Poppy's face, almost too wide to fit. Her mouth was stained red and had Aislin not seen the strawberry seeds stuck between Poppy's teeth, she would've mistaken it for blood.

She was still in the same clothes from school—that pristine white dress and her shiny black ballet flats—but her once unruly hair had been braided into two pigtails. All the while, her eyes never left Aislin's. It was like she was looking for something, or waiting for Aislin to see something that only Poppy knew was there. Sometimes, Aislin forgot that Poppy was Pastor Freel's daughter. They were so wholly different: Poppy with her warm brown hair and round eyes so dark they were almost black looked nothing like Pastor Freel with his white-blonde hair and bright green eyes.

One of her sisters pinched Aislin's thigh. She jumped and turned around. Mavis' eyes narrowed at her and pointed to the pulpit. Pastor Freel settled himself in front of the congregation and began the service.

Aislin grabbed the book with the songs and prayers, cradling it in her lap. She went through the motions: singing, standing, kneeling, singing, standing, kneeling. It was all so tedious, from the hymns she mouthed along to the prayers she recited but never really meant.

"I heard she was adopted." Someone whispered into her ear.

Aislin glanced over her shoulder to find one of her classmates,

Bethany, pointing at Poppy. She hadn't actually whispered it to Aislin. Bethany had leaned towards a friend she was sitting with, Tabitha, but it had felt like she meant the words for Aislin. "After the Freel's *real* daughter died, they replaced her with that...*thing*. It's the only story that makes sense."

The Freel's had lived in Devil's Pointe their entire lives. According to the stories Aislin heard whispered between classes and written on notes passed between hands, Poppy—the *real* Poppy had been born stillborn. Not a wail was to be heard on the hospital floor, save for Mrs. Freel's whimpers. They thought Poppy was dead, but it wasn't until the nurses had taken her to the NICU that she had come to. Some people think that the nurse was a faerie who had replaced the Freel's Poppy with the Poppy currently sitting only a few church pews away.

"I can't imagine anyone would willingly adopt her," Tabitha said. "Didn't you hear she eats animals in the woods by her grandmother's grave? Mary Anne told me she saw her doing it."

Aislin heard a small gasp, and she could only imagine Bethany covered her mouth in surprise. "That's disgusting. But I guess it makes sense. Animals do what animals do."

Tabitha giggled, "She'll be sent off to the Farm soon enough. Then we won't have to look at her anymore."

Aislin never understood why so many people hated Poppy. She rarely spoke, seldom did much of anything besides take walks through the cemetery. The gossips in this town were like vultures, devouring all the filth and carrion in the streets only to spew it back up for the starving masses. She imagined Bethany twirling the pencil she used to take notes in her church diary. It was this ridiculous, gaudy thing covered in pink and green glitter that covered her fingertips every time she used it. Aislin wanted her to take that stupid pencil and shove it into her stupid face so she would stop talking. She imagined the way the sharpened point would slice through the thin skin of her cheek like butter, before blood pooled down the side of her face. She wondered what it would taste like. Wondered what her skin would taste like.

Aislin shook those thoughts out of her head and forced her attention to return to the service. She fiddled with her fingers, locking and interlacing them together to ease her mind away from Bethany and her blood. It was wrong to think things as sinful as that, especially within the house of God. If Mavis ever heard the thoughts Aislin had, she'd send her away to Pastor Freel's farm and Aislin certainly did not want that. All the girls in Devil's Pointe who walked alongside trouble got sent to the farm, but they never came back the same—if they came back at all.

The light from the setting sun poured into the room, casting long shadows across the floor and flooding the room in shades of red and green and blue from the stained-glass windows as a scream pierced through the church. Jesus on the cross, John the Baptist's severed head, Delilah as she cut Samson's hair—they all watched as the congregation fell silent before panic erupted.

Aislin jumped out of her seat and turned around, only to find Bethany with her stupid pink and green glitter pencil through her cheek. She sat sobbing and wailing in her seat, her tears mixing with the blood pouring from her wound. The pencil bobbed around in her mouth like a salmon swimming up a waterfall. Exactly as Aislin had wanted it to happen.

Bethany turned her eyes on Aislin, frantically pointing her finger at her and waving her arms around, as if she knew.

Somehow, she knew. Bethany tried to speak, but her words came out garbled. Saliva and blood dripping out of her mouth and staining her pretty, pink dress. There was a certain prettiness in disgust and if Aislin hadn't been so scared, she might have thought the scene before her was beautiful.

Pastor Freel ran over to help Bethany. Aislin scrambled out of her seat and tripped over her feet trying to get away. A soft pair of arms wrapped around Aislin, stopping her fall.

Bethany kept glaring at Aislin as she pawed at her face, trying to staunch the bleeding with little more than her own fingers. Her friend Tabitha stared at her in shock, utterly frozen in her seat. Most of the congregation had fallen silent, save for the few toddlers and babies that had been frightened half to death by all the screaming.

"It's okay," Poppy whispered into Aislin's hair. "I know you didn't mean to do it."

She looked at Aislin like she knew every thought that had ever crossed her mind. Looked at her like she knew that Aislin wanted Bethany to stab herself. She hadn't meant for Bethany to get hurt, not like this. She just wanted Bethany to stop talking.

Poppy brushed her fingers through Aislin's hair, shushing her like a babe. No one paid them any mind as they held one another amongst the commotion. "It was an accident. It isn't your fault."

The girls watched as Pastor Freel picked up Bethany and rushed her out of the church to his car. Aislin knew Bethany would be fine. She had to be. It was just her cheek.

"Sometimes I have so many thoughts running through my head that they just spill out like melted wax from a candle; and it stains everything around me before I can stop it."

Aislin let Poppy's words wash over her. *It was an accident. They just spill out.* She focused on the softness of her voice, the delicate feeling of her hands through Aislin's hair that reminded her of her dead father. And for the first time in a long time— for the first time since she buried her father in a plot on the opposite side of the cemetery from her mother—Aislin prayed. Prayed that Bethany would be ok. Prayed that Poppy kept holding her. Prayed that no one would find out about what happened. Prayed that it would never happen again.

But Aislin knew it was futile. Her prayers always went unanswered, and God wouldn't save her if he couldn't bother to hear her.

After that day, Aislin could feel Poppy's wide eyes on her even when she couldn't see her, but they never spoke, not until Breena and Vivien had come along. They'd simply watch one another when they thought no one was paying attention, dark eyes peering through stringy curtains of hair. It had become something of a game for them. There was never a moment where they weren't circling one another, like wolves trailing after their prey, never knowing when the other was going to bite.

Aislin - Present

The car managed the rest of the drive up to the cabin. There hadn't been much damage beyond a few dents and scrapes from where her car's front had hit the poor animal. Jamie kept quiet after they got back into the car. The doe had shaken him, so he kept his attention trained on the forest, recording the trees passing them by as they drove in silence.

Aislin imagined the way he would use those clips of the forest to add a darker ambiance to his documentary. She liked the forest surrounding them, the way its calming air soothed her skin and the way its eyes never left her.

When the pair had finally pulled up to the cabin, the usual lights that flooded out from the windows weren't on and the front door was locked. Vivien hadn't arrived yet. It was strange for Aislin to be the first one to make it and she clumsily dug through her bag looking for the keys so she could open the door.

"Sorry, Vivien's always the first to get here."

"You guys have a hierarchy for who shows up to the cabin first?" Jamie chuckled.

Aislin shook her head and brushed her hair away from her face, "No, no nothing like that. It's just that Vivien lives the closest. She moved somewhere near town so she could be close to her mom. She's a writer so she gets to live wherever she wants." She got the door open and the two walked inside.

The air in the cabin was stale—the old scent of lemongrass and bergamot was replaced with the overwhelming stench of mothballs and mildew. It hadn't smelled the same after Poppy disappeared. Even after all these years, the smell hit her like a punch to the gut. Everything else was exactly as it had always been. The old brown leather couches still sat in the living room in front of the now dusty fireplace. Old cream curtains fluttered throughout the room from a draft Aislin couldn't find.

"Where do you and Breena live?"

"Not too far. Breena moved to the city to jump-start her photography gig and I rented a studio just a few towns over so I could work on my paintings for this really uppity art gallery that reached out to me after we became these true crime micro-celebrities." Somehow, a couple of her old art projects from school had made their way onto the internet and the gallery had fallen in love as soon as they saw them. She had painted an entire collection *inspired by what had happened to them in the woods* and made a pretty penny when the gallery sold them. She brought in money, so they didn't care that she rarely showed up for the showcases or events they hosted.

Aislin set her bag down by the door and went about opening a few of the windows to let in the fresh night air. Summer nights were always colder up in the mountains, but the air inside the cabin was stifling. Here and there, large chunks of the white paint were peeling off the windowpanes, revealing the old rotting wood beneath it. Aislin ran her fingers over a particularly large patch and wondered if they would ever get around to painting over it.

The last time the girls had made the trip up here they hadn't been too focused on cleaning. A thick layer of dust adorned every surface and the bundles of wildflowers Vivien had spent an entire afternoon picking had wilted; the dried remains of the fallen petals sat circling the vases. There were old, dusty paintings hanging on every wall that Poppy had either found or painted herself—she had even scattered around a few of Aislin's paintings, Vivien's poems, and Breena's photographs. They were all encased in withered light brown frames.

Poppy, for as wild as she was, liked order. She liked matching color palettes to the seasons, liked having all her pencils the same length, and the way the four of them all had the same round eyes so dark they were almost black, the same wild, untamable hair that all the adults in their lives admonished. She liked the way they were all the exact same height and that they could all share clothes and shoes and jewelry. Poppy had once said to them that they were a perfect matching set.

Poppy's heart still lived and breathed within the cabin. It bore the weight of so many memories in its old, mottled wood panels and while the Freels shied away from it, the girls embraced it. At the cabin, they could pretend Poppy was still with them. They could pretend they heard her humming as she stoked the fire or laughing in the kitchen as she cooked. They could pretend she was laid out in front of the fire, telling them stories of the monsters that stalked through the woods just outside.

"I saw some of your art online. It's some pretty gruesome stuff." She had always been fascinated by the dark and that fascination bled into her work as easy as breathing.

Aislin picked off an already peeling piece of paint and watched as it fluttered to the floor, ignoring the way heat rose to her cheeks. "I guess it is, yeah. But gruesome is subjective."

Once the cabin had cooled a bit, she showed Jamie to his room. She thought of leaving him alone so he could unpack his things, but he followed her right out of the room so they could continue their interview before Breena and Vivien showed up.

He wanted to sit in the living room, but the moment his hands grabbed Poppy's old crochet blanket to move it off the couch, Aislin suggested they go outside. They had never invited anyone else on their yearly trips to the cabin and it was hard to not feel like her space was being invaded, as if he were a rat running along the baseboards. It was still too hot inside for her to feel comfortable anyways.

"So, your dad dies, Poppy shows up. Vivien moves to town, Poppy shows up. Breena starts school, Poppy shows up. But what drew her to you? None of you ever talk about that. You guys all live pretty mysterious lives despite how famous you all have become." He said famous with the same tone someone would use while telling an inside joke.

Aislin shook her head in response, stilling the porch swing as she sat down, "I don't really know. Part of me thinks it was because she was simply there. Another part of me thinks it was fate—that these invisible strings were tying us all together the entire time." She paused to gather her thoughts, "Poppy had found us when we were nothing more than ghosts walking through Devil's Pointe. We all tried so hard to be invisible, to hide in the shadows so no one would notice us. But Poppy demanded the attention from everyone in the room the moment she entered. We had all gotten so used to our solitude that we didn't want to leave it. But Poppy was always just waiting for one of us to take the bait; and every time we ignored her, told her to go away, screamed at her to leave us alone, it only emboldened her. Made her try even harder to get us to crack."

"Why?" Jamie asked.

That was always the question, wasn't it? Why them? What had made them so special? What did Poppy see that no one else did? What no one knew was that Poppy had always been good at finding the things that wanted to stay hidden in the dark.

Though she knew the answer now, Aislin used to spend hours staring up at the cracks and spiderwebs on her ceiling asking herself exactly that.

"Poppy thought we were special. I guess she saw something in us that she felt matched whatever was inside her."

You're not like everyone else in this town—you're more special than you know. You might not realize it now, but someday soon you will. And when that day comes, you'll crawl right into my arms, just like that day in church.

Even more than liking order, Poppy liked knowing things others didn't. She hoarded secrets like a demon collecting the souls of sinners.

And she had been right. Aislin did crawl right to Poppy when whatever was inside had scared her. Just like Breena did, and just like Vivien after her.

"We didn't really all become friends until the school year started. Poppy hounded after us for the entire summer, but it wasn't until the spring formal that any of us really took her seriously."

Jamie cocked his head, like an owl or a wolf, "Took her seriously?"

"Poppy was the preacher's daughter. The town may have thought her strange but because of her father, she was leagues above the rest of us. It didn't really make sense—for Poppy to want to be friends with us. We just didn't get it. And Poppy was always so odd it wasn't like you could figure out her motivations just by watching her. So we played this game of cat and mouse until we reached our boiling points."

"And that was the school dance?"

Aislin nodded her head, eyes watching the trees swaying in the gentle breeze, "I hadn't been allowed to go. Mavis didn't like me going out too much—thought I'd cause trouble for her or her girls. But for whatever reason, that night I ignored her. I put on this pretty vintage dress my mom had worn when she was around my age. It was a little long so I pinned what I could. I grabbed my school shoes and climbed out my window."

"What made you wanna go?"

Aislin shrugged, "I didn't plan it or anything. A boy had asked me to be his date a few days earlier, but I had told him no. It wasn't until a few hours before the dance that I started digging through my mom's old stuff. I found that dress and something told me that I had to go—if only to see what it was like. It was the last dance of the school year, and I didn't want to start eighth grade off feeling like a loser. I just wanted to do…something. Anything. So, I figured the dance would be as good a rebellion as any.

"All in all, it was kind of lame. Nothing like I had hoped, though that probably had more to do with me not having many friends. And the fact that I had to spend most of the night hiding from my sisters. The music was too loud and there were too many people moving and shouting. I didn't even get to dance with the boy who asked me. It probably wasn't a very good idea to use a middle school dance as my entrance into the realm of teenagedom.

"I stood just haunting this corner of the room that I had claimed for myself. Breena, Vivien, and I were all at opposite ends from one another—all watching each other watch Poppy. Compared to us, she had spent most of the night fluttering around the room in this glittery blue dress. We watched her dance and laugh and sing along to the terribly cheap DJ." Aislin had thought she looked like a butterfly flying from flower to flower in a garden. Poppy had braided random strands of her hair and smeared her eyelids in an electric purple shadow. Looking back, Aislin could recognize that Poppy looked a haphazard mess, but through her child eyes, Poppy looked radiant, ethereal.

Poppy embodied everything Aislin hoped to be and everything she wouldn't become. Because while Poppy could twirl around the center of a room full of people who hated her, Aislin shrank into the shadows. She cared too much. Cared about the whispers and the stares and the way everyone's thoughts seemed to buzz around her like flies swarming a piece of rotting meat.

"We had this thing—the Flower Queen. I never paid much attention to that kind of stuff. It seemed so unimportant to me after losing my dad, but my sisters talked about it all the time. They were always trying so hard to get voted as the Flower Queen, but luck was never on their side. Especially not that year." Aislin sighed.

Jamie stared at her with an odd sort of expression, "Why not?"

Aislin cleared her throat and stared down at her hands, fidgeting with her hangnail. "Usually, the most popular girl was crowned Flower Queen. My sisters may have had more friends than me, but they were most definitely not popular."

"Do you remember who got voted that year?"

She chuckled, "Of course I do. It was Poppy. I remember she

was so confused. She almost didn't go on stage to get crowned. Something told me to stop her. But I had chalked it up to me being a bit jealous or sad or angsty. I don't know. So I ignored it—watched her walk up on stage with this beaming smile and despite the ominous feeling churning in my gut, I was happy for her. She looked happy. She was given her flower crown and a little bouquet, and she couldn't stop smiling. It was adorable."

"So was your intuition wrong?" Jamie asked.

Aislin shook her head, "A teenage girl's intuition is never wrong. I was just worried about the wrong thing. After the queen was crowned, everyone would pair up and circle around her on the dance floor. I wanted to join but there was something special about just watching her. Watching her hair whip around her face while she giggled under the disco ball. I can't remember if Breena and Vivien joined in the circle, but I definitely didn't. Before we became friends, I never wanted to invade her space. I let her into mine, of course I let her into mine. But I never asked to be let into hers, so it felt wrong trying to insert myself somewhere she might not want me." Aislin's voice trailed off as she thought about the memory.

"I guess Poppy was spinning so much that she got sick, and she had to excuse herself to the bathroom. That was when the bad feeling came back. This girl Bethany and a group of her friends followed Poppy out after a few minutes. I tried convincing myself that I was just being dramatic. Bethany had a mean streak, and she really didn't like Poppy."

"Why not?" Jamie liked to jump at any opportunity to find out why someone didn't like Poppy. He was like a slobbering dog trying to bite at a bone.

"Girls are always pit against one another. If it isn't our teachers or parents, it's ourselves. But we didn't actually hate each other, not really. We were all just like mirrors for one another and we all hated what we saw staring back at us, not the actual girl."

Every girl was always looking at every other girl's hair, blouse, shined church shoes, clear nail polish, pink nail polish, red nail polish (only if she was a slut), black nail polish (only if she was a satanist), tasteful amount of mascara (too much made you look trashy, but not enough made you look lazy), silver jewelry, gold jewelry, backpack, purses, posture, stomach, arm, cheekbones—the list never ended. It was easier to pick apart another girl when you already knew what you were looking for.

"Anyways, I finally mustered up the courage to walk out into the hallway. Breena and Vivien must have been thinking the same thing because they walked out only a few seconds after me. I could kind of hear the girls' voices echoing down the hall, but I didn't really know where they were. Everything was so muffled because of the music, and I got a bit turned around. Vivien knew exactly where to go though. She practically sprinted down the hallway to the bathroom.

"When we got to the door, we could hear some thudding and giggling, whispers. We peaked in, too scared to just push open the door, and saw Poppy on the floor. Her nose was gushing blood, and she had this awful cut across her eyebrow. All the girls around her were kicking her, slapping her, pulling her hair. It was awful. They did anything and everything to keep her on the ground and she was bleeding so much that it was starting to spill onto the tile. The three of us were completely frozen. I don't know what was more horrifying: the way the girls were all laughing to themselves as they beat Poppy up or the way Poppy barely made a sound." *Like she was used to the feeling of someone's foot in her ribs.*

Aislin told Jamie about how the girls broke up the fight and got the school nurse to take care of Poppy. She told him about how the three girls huddled around her too and helped clean the blood off her swollen cheek and busted lip. She told him about how they laughed when Poppy lamented the fact that she would probably not be able to wear that dress again because of all the blood stains on it.

But Aislin didn't tell Jamie that her mouth watered at the sight of the blood. It was wrong, she knew that, but she couldn't help it at the time. She didn't tell him that her mind went fuzzy when Bethany split the skin on her knuckle from punching Poppy. She didn't tell him that she bit Bethany's shoulder to get her to get stop, to get her away from Poppy. She especially did not tell him about how much she enjoyed the taste of Bethany's skin on her tongue, how her blood tasted as sweet as vanilla ice cream on a hot summer day. She didn't tell Jamie that she had bit off a small piece of Bethany's shoulder, savored the feel of it in her mouth. Not even Bethany told anyone about that.

Secrets had to be kept. Only Poppy and the girls got the privilege of knowing her secrets.

Besides, the story she told him wasn't too far from the truth.

But the way Jamie looked at her, it was like he knew everything that was unspooling inside her head. He raised his eyebrow at her as if he didn't quite believe her version of the tale. He waited, with bated breath, for Aislin to finish the story.

Under the scrutiny of his gaze, Aislin flinched, that familiar curl of shame expanding in her stomach. Aislin didn't mean to bite Bethany as hard as she did. But something had come over her when her lips met with flesh. She had become this starved, rabid animal the moment the first drop of blood had hit her tongue. It was a headrush and for the first time in her life, Aislin's mind went blank. There was no fight, no. There was only her and the blood in her mouth and the body of Bethany in her arms.

She had expected Breena and Vivien to react the same way as Bethany, to run far away from her screaming and crying. But they hadn't. Breena had rested her hand on Aislin's shoulder and brushed her fingers over Aislin's now messy hair. Vivien had wiped the blood off of Aislin's chin with her thumb and licked it clean. When Aislin looked at them, at Breena and Vivien and Poppy, that same hunger simmering under her skin lingered in their eyes.

After the school nurse found them and helped clean up Poppy, the girls had all sat together outside. They all interlaced their fingers and leaned against one another. Something had changed that night.

For the first time in her life, Aislin had a friend. Three friends.

Aislin shook off his eyes and turned her gaze back to the tree line, "At any other school Bethany would have been expelled for what she did. But Devil's Pointe only has one school, so her only other option was the Farm." Between the church incident and the stunt she pulled at the dance, her parents and the Freels decided to quietly send her off to the Farm. Aislin would sometimes overhear the whispers that followed Bethany's name throughout the school halls and the church pews. "The town had thought her possessed so they kept her corralled for as long as they could."

For a while, neither of them spoke. She could tell that Jamie wanted to press her for more information, but he must have thought better of it because he simply asked, "Did that happen often? Possession?" A small chuckle followed his question. A smirk graced his face, as if he didn't really believe her.

Aislin shrugged; the soft breeze of the mountains twirled her hair around its fingers. She didn't bother brushing it away from her face, "In a small town like Devil's Pointe demons are always just around the corner. I suppose possession is easier to handle than a psychotic break. And sometimes, girls just break. There isn't always a reason and the town just couldn't understand that."

Jamie stared off into the darkness of the forest. Something akin to confusion crossed his face, but it vanished just as quickly as it had appeared. Aislin turned her own eyes to the tree line but found nothing but the slight sway of the trees.

Poppy used to say that if you stared at the shadows for long enough, they'd come to life. Snake and slither their way closer and closer towards you, until you couldn't stop them. It had scared Aislin at first, but she knew that it was just another of Poppy's stories. The same stories her father used to tell her.

Jamie settled his attention back on Aislin, "You've mentioned that place a few times now—the Farm. What is it? Some kind of summer camp?"

Aislin stiffened at the question. It was innocent. Anyone would question her about what the Farm was if it was brought up. Though she had moved away from Devil's Pointe, the town still had its claws in her. No one spoke of the Farm. Not directly. It was always a hidden threat from a parent when their kid was getting into trouble, a whispered secret passed between lips smeared in strawberry lip gloss.

She shrugged her shoulders, "It was just this patch of land the Freels owned. It's where all the wayward girls would get sent away and Pastor Freel would put them to work taking care of the land. It's just down the road from here, but after Poppy's death, her father shut it all down. The three of us could take you to see it in the morning if you'd like."

Aislin didn't like the idea of taking Jamie to the Farm. It was personal. The place of her hurt and her salvation. But Jamie seemed all too pleased to visit and Aislin didn't exactly know how to tell him no.

"What landed the four of you at the Farm?" His voice wavered—the first sign of apprehension—but his eyes were wide with curiosity.

Aislin had to stop herself from laughing. She knew what he was really asking. What he wanted to ask. And she knew the ways her answer would be carved apart and twisted to fit whatever narrative the audience wants. She had seen the tabloids plastered in every grocery store and gas station, read through the subreddits trying to solve Poppy's disappearance.

There had never been any suspects except for the Lambs themselves—Aislin, Breena, and Vivien. There wasn't a corner of the internet or the media or the world that didn't think they were at least partly responsible for Poppy. But there wasn't any evidence. No body had ever been found.

His eyes watched her through the viewfinder, as if he were too scared to look at her directly. Aislin had gotten used to the stares—or lack thereof. Some people stared too long, others tried too hard to not stare at all. Jamie was the latter.

Had he even looked at her once since they met? Or had he only kept her in his periphery, daring glimpses at her every time he worked up the nerve? She could sense the rapid rise and fall of his chest that he tried to steady, could almost hear the uneven pounding of heart as it thudded against his ribs as he waited for her answer.

Aislin kept picking at her hangnail. "We broke. Every girl in Devil's Pointe did eventually. Going off the deep end and ending up at the Farm was practically a rite of passage. You can only keep bending and bending and bending for so long before you snap right in half, leaving you broken and bloodied for all to see." Aislin paused, mulling over her words. She stared up at the now dark sky and watched the too far away stars blink down at her, as if they were the eyes of God himself. "That's what it was like living in that town, being pushed and bent and snapped until you couldn't take it anymore. Poppy was the only one that made it bearable."

"What about Breena and Vivien?" Jamie's voice was lighter now, a small smile toying at his mouth, as he looked her in the eyes for the first time that night.

Had he not been prying into their private lives, had he been anyone else, Aislin might have thought him handsome with his soft brown hair and wide blue eyes. But there was something underneath them, something lying in wait just under the surface. She felt it in the way his eyes lingered at the hair sitting on her neck, the way his eyes slowly trailed a line over her arms and down to her hands where they sat on the tops of her thighs. Now that he had looked at her in the soft, yellow glow of the porch light, she didn't know if he would look away. If he would try to hide that look of hunger.

Aislin shook those thoughts away, forcing her attention back to his question. "Poppy held us all together, without her, I don't think any of us would be much of anything. She still does. We feel her in the air around us after a rainstorm. We see her in our own reflections when we look at ourselves in the mirror. She's the tie that connects us all together."

Jamie's mouth stayed shut, his eyes still raking over her body, as he waited for her to tell him more.

"She met us when we all needed someone to help carry our pain and Poppy had always been more than happy to do it. After my father died, Poppy never let me out of her sight. Breena's grandmother had just stopped homeschooling her and the kids at school had been brutal, so Poppy started keeping an eye on her too. She and her grandmother had always been pariahs—never went to church, never participated in the fairs or fundraisers. And when Vivien became the town outlander after moving to Devil's Pointe, Poppy did the same thing for her."

"There's something I've been meaning to ask you, but I don't want you to take it the wrong way." Jamie interjected.

Aislin flinched. Careful. He was so careful with the way he questioned her. Just like how she was so careful when answering those questions.

She shrugged her shoulders, "I'll try my best to answer whatever it is you want to know."

Jamie hesitated a moment, his eyes searching her for any signs of doubt. "What did she taste like?"

Aislin startled; eyes wide as she whipped around to face him. While she could feel the wild, unrestrained surprise on her face, Jamie's face was a blank canvas of cool, calm. He was damn near unreadable.

"Who?" Aislin knew who. But she wanted him to say it.

"Bethany. What did she taste like?"

Jamie brought his eyes to hers as he assessed her—his eyes still lazily dragging across her face. He shouldn't have known about that. Had someone told him? Had he guessed? Why would he want to know? The look of disdain or even disgust that Aislin had expected to find on his face, was nowhere to be found. Instead, his eyes were glimmering with an insatiable curiosity that nearly matched Poppy's.

"Excuse me?"

"I heard you bit her so hard you tore a chunk of her shoulder off. You must have tasted her right?"

Aislin picked at the skin around her thumb. "I don't want to talk about that."

Jamie nodded, his eyes soft, but Aislin didn't miss the flash of annoyance that crossed his face. "That's ok. What do you want to talk about?"

But before Aislin could respond, his attention was snatched away from her as bright lights flashed through the dark. Aislin thanked whatever was watching over her in that moment as she heard the blessed sound of a car coming up the driveway.

The engine was killed, the car doors opened, and out stepped Breena and Vivien. They looked as gorgeous as ever. As Aislin watched the two girls rounding the front of the car, she understood why so many people mistook them all for sisters. Breena with her wild curly hair so blonde it was almost white and Vivien with her hair dark as the night sky looming over them looked so different, yet their faces both held the same too large dark eyes, small noses, and sharp jawlines. Aislin knew if she looked in the mirror, she too would find those exact same features staring back at her.

Jamie stared at the girls with wide eyes, before clearing his throat and standing up. He angled his camera to get a better shot of the girls as they walked up the driveway towards the porch and Vivien narrowed her eyes at him.

"Hope we aren't interrupting any important footage," Breena said, her eyes narrowed as she smiled at the pair. She had this way of looking at you that made you forget what you were thinking about.

Jamie quickly shook his head, "Not at all. We were actually just finishing up."

Vivien kept staring at him, her soft eyes assessing him as he stood before them. On the outside, he looked calm, almost bashful, but Aislin heard the heady thump of his heart and the way his lips trembled as her friend continued her look over of him. She watched Jamie the way she watched everyone. They stood there for what seemed like hours, just staring and staring back, until Vivien's full lips parted. Compared to the rest of the girls, her softness was always alarming.

"We should probably head inside. It's going to get cold soon."

Breena - Present

Sometimes, the story started with Breena Doherty. Breena had always been the most hesitant around Poppy, rejecting her kindness and offers of friendship at every turn, but now she was the most protective of her. Though Vivien and Aislin were all too happy to help this Jamie kid with his documentary, Breena had been less than thrilled at the prospect of having him invade their space for the weekend. She had been hesitant around everyone really; her grandmother, Shannon, had been a paranoid woman and she had forced that paranoia down Breena's throat until she choked.

Always be on your guard in this town. Never let anyone think you're weak or you'll be the Devil's poppet.

She heard those words whispered to her on the wind as she watched Jamie grab his camera. His hands shook just the slightest amount, giving away his nervousness.

He held up that ridiculous camera to the girls, ushering Aislin into the frame so he could get a shot of all of them together, though it felt awkward and too forced. Breena fought the urge to roll her eyes at his amateur camerawork. Wasn't he supposed to be some rising star in the indie film world? Didn't he know how to use a camera?

Vivien hid her giggle behind a delicate hand, clearly just as unimpressed by him as Breena. He was clumsy, nearly dropping it out of his hands as he moved to follow Vivien into the cabin.

Holding a camera was like second nature for her. Jamie just looked like an idiot. Maybe he normally hired other people to film while he directed. He looked like the kind of man that enjoyed telling people what to do while he just watched. Typical.

As Aislin turned to walk inside, Breena grabbed her arm to stop her. She waited until the door gently closed behind Jamie before talking.

"How did it go?"

Aislin was on edge, but there was a spark in her eyes that loosened Breena's own worry. Only slightly.

Aislin glanced up at the cabin, as if worried he might hear them, "It went fine. But I think he's spoken to someone from Devil's Pointe about us."

"What did he say?" Breena followed Aislin's gaze, taking in the old, rotting wood of the cabin. She was surprised that it hadn't fallen apart yet, but it made sense. Poppy had loved this cabin as viciously as she loved the girls. Even in death, Breena doubted Poppy would let it fall to ruin.

Aislin shrugged. "His questions were so careful, until—" Her voice drifted off in the wind.

At that Breena raised an eyebrow, "Until?"

"He asked me about the spring formal, school dances and stuff," Aislin said, but Breena got the feeling Aislin was hiding something. She was always so controlled, so collected on the outside. There had been so few times that Breena had seen Aislin let go of that calm facade. She could see the cracks starting to form. Jamie had gotten under her skin. "But he hasn't asked anything about the incident, so I don't really know what he wants."

That was strange. To ask about a small dance but completely ignore the disappearance of Poppy. Jamie hadn't looked like the patient type. Maybe Breena had been wrong, maybe they had all been wrong, but that rarely ever happened. But maybe it was possible he didn't care about the incident as much as they had assumed he would. Maybe he just wanted to make some stupidly aesthetic documentary about their healing journey and other bullshit.

"That's why I think he's already met with someone from town. He isn't itching to figure us out because he already knows something."

"Who the hell would he have talked to?" The people of Devil's Pointe had too many of their own secrets to risk talking to an outsider about anyone else's. It was what kept the town so safe. So private. They were the insiders, and the rest of the world were the outsiders. "That whole town might hate us, but they aren't stupid. Implicating us implicates everyone else tenfold."

Aislin didn't answer, instead choosing to wrap her arms around her middle. Behind them, the trees rustled with the wind, bending under the weight pressing against it. The scent of rain filled the air and soon the scent of damp earth would follow. Breena could feel eyes watching them from the shadows, but she refused to turn around. Whatever it was meant no harm. She had been held under the microscope in Devil's Point for long enough to know when someone watching her wanted to hurt her. It was just sitting, observing, waiting, and it could stay there for all Breena cared.

"I don't like them being alone in the cabin together."

Aislin laughed and rolled her eyes, "You and I both know Vivien is more than capable of protecting herself. You're just being overprotective."

Breena grabbed her hand, and together they walked inside.

Vivien had put on a record and Breena let the noise soothe her anxiety as she closed the door behind her. She liked listening to the pops and crackles of the record player more than the actual music.

Vivien stood over the stove in the kitchen making tea while Jamie sat at the little kitchen table by the bay window. Breena thought back to those slow mornings she would spend with Poppy watching the sunrise. She rarely ever slept through the night; no matter what time she went to bed, she always woke up before the sunrise. And when they were at the cabin, she'd always find Poppy sitting in the bay window—a pot of coffee already brewed on the counter, buttered toast sitting on the table.

She had never seen Poppy sleep. She was always awake and alert, watching and waiting. For what, Breena had no idea. But that was always how Poppy liked things.

Breena rarely sat in the bay window anymore, but she still felt intensely protective of it and seeing Jamie sitting so close to it felt wrong. Seeing him in the goddamned cabin felt wrong. He wasn't supposed to be here. He was an outsider trying to pry into their lives and Breena wanted nothing to do with it.

But she would go along with it to appease Vivien.

It was one small sacrifice and Breena was willing to do much worse for her girls. It's what you did for the people you cared about. Breena never understood the way love was portrayed in the movies. It was always so soft, like some kind of beautiful, docile thing. But her love wasn't selfless or pure, no matter how badly she wanted it to be. It was a bloody and selfish creature that tore through her body like barbed wire. It took and it took and it gave and it gave until there was nothing left but skin dried to bone.

Whatever Aislin and Vivien wanted Breena would give it to them. She'd gouge her own eyes out from her head if they asked her to, and they would do the same.

It had been a year since they were all together, and her heart lurched at the sight of Vivien cooking in the kitchen as Aislin rifled through the cabinets to find something. Despite all the years they spent here, Aislin still couldn't remember how Poppy organized things. Poppy should have been the fourth in their little group, not Jamie. She should be the one following them around and asking uncomfortable questions and talking in riddles.

Her absence had been akin to the feeling of a popsicle melting all over your fingers in the summer heat, sticky and sickly sweet. But with Jamie taking up the space Poppy once occupied, Breena felt nauseated. She wanted to pick up that cutting board Vivien was using and bash it over his head until the sound of his annoyingly erratic heartbeat left her ears.

Breena took a deep breath and sat down, watching as Vivien and Aislin made sandwiches for everyone. Breena always had been a lousy cook, far better outside the kitchen than in it. Shannon hadn't ever trusted her at the stove.

"I told Jamie that he can interview you next," Vivien said as she grabbed the teacups from the cabinet. "I figured you wouldn't mind."

She sent Breena a soft, knowing smile. Better to get it over with sooner rather than later. It wasn't that she hated the boy, but there was something off about him. The way his eyes roamed, hungry and wanting. He reminded her of every little boy that tried to steal a kiss from her or pulled on her hair.

Aislin set down the plates at the table—placing one in front of Breena—before sitting down and grabbing a plate for herself. Breena and Vivien had only had enough time to stop by the small convenience store just outside of town to pick up some bread and cheese. They hadn't run into anyone they knew, but there had been a group of young girls that looked a little too much like Aislin, Breena, Vivien, and Poppy when they had been teens.

Four girls giggling and running around, completely untouchable to the rest of the world. They had been wearing white dresses and skating around on rollerblades.

Poppy had bought them all rollerblades the first Christmas they spent together and once the snow had cleared, they skated everywhere. It was an odd facade of freedom. The feeling of the wind in their hair, the speed of the trees blurring by. They could go anywhere. Do anything. At least that's what it felt like but for the time, it was enough.

None of the girls had looked at Breena and Vivien for long enough to recognize them, which she supposed she was thankful for. It was weird enough that the girls had become so infamous online, even weirder that they had become some kind of Devil's Pointe folktale. It made sense though, four girls vanished in the woods and were presumed dead for months, until one day, three of them miraculously reappeared. She knew stories of them had grown and morphed into legend.

They were weird girls in life and even weirder girls in myth.

It had almost made her smile when she realized that there were other young girls that saw them and looked up to them. Vivien had been busy grabbing the bread and when she looked up at the group of them standing in front of the slushie machine, she had paused and stared in bewilderment. She had looked confused, almost startled. Maybe she hadn't thought about the way others would react to what had happened.

Breena herself hadn't taken a lot of time to think about their return to Devil's Pointe—hadn't dwelled on their pristine white dresses or the soothing burn at the back of her throat. She had never dared to look up the pictures, though she imagined how ethereal they must have looked. Like the Maenads. Like the triple goddess made tangible. Aislin had done a whole series depicting the scene. They had been gruesome, abstract paintings and Breena owned prints of every single one.

As the girls ate their sandwiches, they could hear Jamie rustling around in the room, his soft, murmuring voice echoing off the paper-thin walls. Jamie had left to settle into the guest room right off the kitchen. His camera had died, and he needed to upload the footage onto his computer. Aislin had gone in after some time to give him the sandwich they had made.

As the girls busied themselves with cleaning up the kitchen, Vivien pressed a kiss to the top of Breena's head, "We should head to bed. It's getting late."

Breena followed Aislin and Vivien into Poppy's old room. The yellow floral wallpaper had started peeling before Poppy had first brought them all, but now it looked apocalyptic. The flowered designs could only be seen if you pressed your nose to the wall and squinted, faded from sun damage and old age. The frames encasing paintings and sketches and photographs were practically falling off of their hooks. It was as if the walls themselves were rotting with the loss of Poppy.

Aislin went about turning the bed down while Vivien grabbed pajamas for them all to change into. Aislin brushed Breena's hair while Breena braided Vivien's. Breena turned out the lights, bathing the three girls in the moonlight spilling through the window. The three girls climbed into bed, Aislin and Vivien curled up on either side of Breena. The girls always shared Poppy's room. Once they had all found one another, it felt somehow wrong to be apart. Even in sleep they had to feel one another, be as close as possible to one another. It was an insatiable desire so intense, Breena thought one day she might wake up and find herself curled up in the ribcage of one of the other girls.

Breena didn't sleep. She rested her head atop Vivien's dark tangles, inhaling her sandalwood shampoo, while Aislin nuzzled her face against Breena's side like a cat. She imagined Poppy's hand reaching over Aislin to brush through Breena's hair. Imagined Poppy's hand intertwined with Vivien's from across the bed. Poppy's absence was felt like a hole in the chest. None of the girls could ever staunch the bleeding.

The incident had corrupted everything it touched. It was like a leech, latching onto some poor unsuspecting leg that tripped into its pond and suckling away until there was nothing left but bone.

It wasn't until the early morning light filtered through the windows that Breena extracted herself from the girls. She changed into a pair of jeans and brushed her teeth, before quietly wandering out into the hallway.

The cabin was quiet as a tomb—there were no creaking floors or groaning walls. There was nothing but the still morning air and the barely-there lilac of Poppy's perfume.

As Breena rounded the corner to enter the kitchen, she let out a small gasp of surprise as she found Jamie sitting at the table. He leaned his feet up on the bay window and his camera sat right beside him —red light blinking on and off. He clearly was someone who wasn't comfortable with the prospect of missing anything that could be considered "vital footage." She rolled her eyes and ignored him.

Jamie turned to her and offered a small smile, "I made some coffee. I hope that was ok."

It wasn't. Not in the slightest. But Breena couldn't run him out of the cabin yet, not when Vivien had other plans for him. So she bit her tongue and thanked him, ignoring the way her blood heated at the thought of him going through the kitchen cabinets, rustling through drawers and closets he had no fucking business digging in.

She poured a mug for herself but stayed rooted to the counter. She wouldn't sit in the bay window with Jamie at the table. It was too close for her.

"During our interview yesterday, Aislin kept mentioning the Farm?" He phrased it like a question, as if he knew exactly what he was talking about but wanted to lead Breena to the answer herself. *Kill me.*

"Aislin likes to talk about a lot of things." She took a sip of her coffee and held back the gag that threatened to spill out. The coffee was disgusting, and she didn't know if it was because the grounds had gone stale or if Jamie really did taint everything he touched.

Swiping the back of her hand across her mouth, she emptied her mug in the sink and turned back to face him.

Jamie appraised her, taking in her rumbled, oversized sleep shirt, her tangled hair, the bags under her eyes. "I thought we could film your portion of the interview there. Aislin said it wasn't too far from here."

"It's not." Breena shook her head. The Freels had always liked to be close to the Farm in case anything happened. "Just a short walk east." She wasn't going to offer to take him there, but if he asked, she, unfortunately, wouldn't say no.

"We should do your interview there. I like capturing my subjects in isolation. It makes you all stand out better."

Breena scoffed and rolled her eyes, "We can go. It'll give Vivien and Aislin time to spruce up the cabin."

"That works for me," Jamie said. He stood from his seat at the table and Breena made a mental note to leave a note for Vivien to clean it after they were gone. "When do you want—"

"Now." Breena spoke for him. "Let me just get some things; then we can leave." Outside was better. Safer. Farther away from the cabin and her memories of Poppy.

Before Breena could walk back to Poppy's bedroom, Aislin and Vivien joined the pair in the kitchen.

The group was silent until Aislin cleared her throat, "I think it's going to rain soon. Why don't you head to the Farm in the afternoon once it lets up? For now, you can sit in the guest bedroom. Vivien and I will be out here, so you don't have to worry about us eavesdropping."

"You can finally say all the terrible things you've been thinking of us all these years." Vivien smiled.

Breena shoved Vivien's shoulder and stifled the giggle that threatened to bubble up her throat.

"Will that be ok, Breena?" Jamie asked. *How gentlemanly.*

She shook her head. She needed to get out of the cabin and the mere thought of sitting still while being interviewed by the boy made her skin crawl. "We'll be fine at the Farm. If it rains, we'll head inside the caf and I'm sure Jamie has something to protect his *precious* equipment, just in case."

Aislin and Vivien shared a look but didn't press Breena further. Vivien raised her eyebrows in warning. *Behave.* Then she turned on her heel and headed back into Poppy's bedroom.

She trusted Breena to handle herself around Jamie, just like she trusted Aislin to drive up with him.

Their trust in one another was implicit and there wasn't anything in the world that could lead to Breena breaking that trust.

She slipped on her boots and pulled one of Poppy's old coats from the closet, before walking out the door. Her lilac scent enveloped Breena and helped calm her racing heart. No matter how many times they washed Poppy's old clothes, the smell never went away.

Jamie grabbed his camera and followed her outside.

Breena let out a sigh of relief at the feeling of the morning breeze on her too hot skin. She could finally breathe.

Jamie fiddled with his camera before training it on her. "So, where do you want to start?"

"Shouldn't you be asking more pointed questions?" Breena kept her eyes trained on the ground. It was odd, being in front of the camera after spending so much time behind it.

Jamie hummed in acknowledgment, "I prefer giving my subjects the opportunity to be their authentic selves, without interference from me."

Breena snorted, "That's ridiculous. All subjects need direction, otherwise you end up with a whole lot of nonsense. Even with interviews. Surely there's a story you're trying to tell—a narrative you're trying to push." When it came to her photography, she was always pushing her subjects into their poses, shoving them into the frame. They needed to be poked, prodded because they didn't understand the vision, only the one behind the camera knew what the shot was truly supposed to look like.

"And what narrative do you think I'm trying to push?"

A sharp retort sat on the tip of her tongue like a bead of blood after you lick a paper cut on a finger, but Breena kept her mouth closed and decided not to answer. The trees grew denser around them as they walked deeper into the forest. Though she had never been scared of the forest surrounding Devil's Pointe, she had been scared of the Farm. Every girl in town was. Some parents scared their children into behaving with stories of the Boogeyman or the monsters under your bed, but the people of Devil's Pointe scared their girls straight with stories of the Farm. Every mother had been there, every sister, every cousin. Everyone had stories about the way the trees totally covered the light of the moon in the night or the way the earth was deathly silent under their feet. Breena couldn't stop the familiar tingle of fear that shot up her spine as they made their way through the forest.

"What did you and Aislin talk about?"

If Jamie noticed the shift in conversation, he didn't comment on it. "Mostly when you all first became friends—around middle school. You can talk about what it was like growing up together. I'm sure with how small of a community Devil's Pointe is there was bound to be some drama."

"When is there not drama in a teenage girl's life?" Breena thought back to Vivien and the way she had made Breena promise to behave. She bit her tongue and tried her best to answer him. "If I'm being honest, it was a lot easier to handle once we had all become friends. Sure, we were still the town weirdos but at least we weren't loners."

Jamie trained his camera on Breena. She could hear the sharp zoom of the lens and the intake of breath before he asked, "What makes you say you guys were *weirdos?*"

Breena was five seconds away from shoving that camera out

of Jamie's hands. She could only imagine the headache she would get if she watched his shaky footage.

"Weirdos always sounded nicer than freaks. At least it does to me anyways. If you asked Poppy, she'd have preferred *freaks*. She reveled in the town's ostracization of her. According to everyone else, we didn't quite meet their standards of civilization. I was pretty much the only kid that never went to church. Aislin was a goody-two-shoes try hard that never went to parties. Vivien lived with her sinfully unmarried mother and painted her nails black. And Poppy—" Breena paused, chewing on the words in her mouth to get them to come out the way she wanted. "Poppy disturbed a lot of people. She had this way of looking through you, as if she could hear your thoughts. She was a great listener. I don't think there was a secret in Devil's Pointe she didn't know. And in turn, there wasn't a secret *we* didn't know in Devil's Pointe."

Out of the girls, Breena was the most hesitant to talk about Poppy. It wasn't that she thought she'd say the wrong thing—in fact, the girls had spent so much time perfecting their answers and statements that their speech was now eloquent, graceful—but she was scared of saying too much. She held Poppy in the pit of her stomach like a secret and she hated sharing.

"And that upset a lot of people?"

God. Were all his questions going to be this stupid? How did Aislin even make it through her interview?

She rolled her eyes. "Obviously. But we all kept to ourselves. We were completely separated from our parents, teachers, peers—hell, the whole town. There was no way we could be a real threat to anyone."

"Most people only bother learning other people's secrets so they can use it against them."

Breena shook her head, "Not Poppy. She was like a…wishing tree or something. She'd learn secrets and keep them for no other reason besides she liked them. It was the closest thing to intimacy she could get." She nearly regretted saying the last part out loud.

"Until you three came along." He turned in her direction, giving her a pointed look.

Breena nodded, "Until the three of us came along."

Silence hung in the air between them like a swarm of flies on rotting meat. She had a therapist that used to do the same thing. It was supposed to help Breena sit with her emotions and all that garbage, but it did nothing but make her feel uninteresting.

Then, Jamie finally broke the quiet, "What did intimacy mean to you guys?"

Breena let out a loud sigh. If she couldn't verbally berate him, the least she could do was make it known how irritated she was with his moronic questions. "I don't know…sharing or whatever. We had been such solitary creatures for so long, we just wanted to share everything with each other—our space, our time, our secrets, our inconsequential thoughts. Everything. We didn't have to hide from one another."

The Farm wasn't too far away and lucky for them, the terrain remained relatively even the whole way. The Freels had practically carved a path through the forest, tree stumps littered the ground and the grass had never really managed to grow back properly, leaving it dry and yellow.

"You know, Aislin did the same thing in her interview," he said, nearly tripping over an exposed tree root. He managed to catch himself before he fell, much to Breena's chagrin.

"Am I supposed to magically know what you're talking about?" She didn't slow down, just kept walking at her own pace and she could hear his footfalls as he jogged to catch up with her.

"She referred to you guys as *creatures* too. I was just merely pointing out that it's an odd word choice, but Aislin certainly wasn't this abrasive."

Breena scoffed at his dramatics, "*Abrasive?* Am I not answering your questions? You should be content that I'm even doing this interview to begin with. That I'm even taking you to the Farm."

The sheer audacity of him to suggest that she was anything other than cooperative.

"I didn't mean to offend you. It's obvious you're not the biggest fan of doing this."

"Oh, wow, really? Please do tell me more." Vivien's voice nagged at the back of her mind, but Breena couldn't stop.

From where they stood, Breena could almost see the Farm far in the distance.

"You mentioned earlier that I'm pushing a narrative, but you never told me what narrative you thought I was pushing."

Breena shrugged, "You're likely pushing the narrative everyone pushes—we killed Poppy. We hid out in the woods to throw off suspicion, faked our own kidnapping, tied ourselves up like that. I've read all the boards and the posts and the think pieces. They all point fingers, try to find someone to blame, and that someone is always us. And if by some miracle you aren't trying to blame us, then you're trying to blame someone."

"Why do you think that is?"

"We're the easy answer." Breena looked up from the ground and met Jamie's eyes. "A respectable preacher's daughter vanishes into thin air and the only people who were with her can't tell anyone what happened. A young girl presumed dead, her three weird friends never see trial. Every lead went cold, and nothing came of it. The world had been denied their justice and they were angry. So they took it—take it—out on us."

Jamie paused a moment, waiting to see if she would say any more. When she didn't, Jamie asked, "And you think that's what I'm doing?"

"I don't know what you're doing. If that is the angle you're pursuing, it's uninspired. Sure, you have the added intrigue of us talking to you, but that will only take you and your *documentary* so far. So you have to do something to make it special, but I can't predict it. That is why I don't trust you." There were many ways to get there from the Freel cabin—the path, the rocks, the river. But Breena kept on the open pathway. She didn't trust herself to be in such close proximity to him.

Jamie scoffed, "You don't know I'm trying to prove you guys killed her." He looked deeply offended.

"I don't know," Breena mumbled, "But there isn't a single bone in my body waiting for you to prove me wrong."

"And how would I do that?"

"I don't know that either. But you are digging into something you don't understand for the sake of your own entertainment, just like everyone else. So, really, how different could you be?"

"My own entertainment?" Jamie asked, "I'm not even interested in Poppy."

As the words left his mouth, Breena felt her heart stutter. *Not even interested in Poppy?* "Everyone's interested in Poppy. She's the only one who didn't come back." Her throat tightened.

"Not me. I mean sure, I can't deny that Poppy is the catalyst for your stories, but they're your stories. Yours, Aislin's, Vivien's. You're the Lambs—the survivors. You all saw the world through Poppy so of course I have to ask about her."

Breena had always hated the word *survivor* because the truth was, they hadn't survived. They had lost something vital out in those woods and there was nothing any of them could do to get it back. They had lost Poppy in the woods. They had lost themselves. If Poppy hadn't survived and if she hadn't, how could the rest of them? How could they be survivors when their lifeblood had been stolen?

Breena - Middle School

The day Breena's mother left was too bright and too warm. She remembered how the light filtered through the leaves of the trees swaying in the wind, soaring so high above her she thought the sharp branches might have torn a hole right through the sky. Remembered the way her mother's eyes shimmered in the growing sunlight.

It was a normal day. Her mother dressed her for the morning—picked out a pair of shorts and a plain t-shirt two sizes too big, handed her a pair of dirty sneakers and socks, and filled her backpack with her toothbrush and a few books she liked to read. She didn't bother to help Breena brush her hair. It was always so tangled and messy that Breena was never able to fix it herself, but her mother had always loved her hair, no matter how messy. Sometimes, the two would stay up and sit in silence while her mother tied ribbons and pinned barrettes in her hair.

Breena tied her shoelaces into little bunny ears and waited by the door with her backpack. It was new, bright purple and covered in glitter with a little rabbit sitting in the center of it. She rarely was able to get new things, so she took extra special care of it—she would never let it touch the ground, always hung it up on the hook in her closet and whenever it got dirty she made sure to clean it.

Her mother walked over to her, flattening down her hair as she hummed a tune to herself. They both had the same unruly blonde hair and small button nose, but while her mother's eyes were a dull blue, Breena's were nearly black. Her mother always complained about how Breena's eyes grew darker as she grew up, as if there was some entity slowly taking her over. She had always wondered if her father had the same eyes as her, or the same pale skin. Her mother had gorgeous bronze skin that Breena had always been envious of. She was illuminated under the summer sun, while Breena always burned.

Without a word, Breena's mother walked to the door and got inside their rusted old Toyota. Breena followed her out and into the car, settling her backpack into her lap. She didn't ask any questions about why they were leaving the house in the middle of the night, or where they were going. Her mother started the car and pulled out of the driveway, whispering to herself, too soft for Breena to understand.

Everything about her was soft, from the skin on her hands to the creases around her smile. Even her mind was soft. She'd break down in tears while watching a dog commercial or scream and break plates if Breena upset her. With her mother, it was like having both a marble statue and a feral cat in her home.

Breena had been her mother's miracle child. She had kept Breena's baby scrapbook hidden under the floorboards in her bedroom. Every page was filled with photos of her beside angels and prayer letters written by her mother, begging God to give her a child. Her prayers had been answered, but for some reason, Breena's mother hadn't been too happy with the child she had been given.

Her mother didn't speak much, she mostly just walked through the house singing under her breath or mumbling incoherently. She loved music though she never played anything. Their house was always so quiet. Full of nothing but creaking stairs and groaning walls. Sometimes, if she stayed up late enough or when she woke up just before the sun rose, she could hear her mother dancing in the living room and singing the words to an old song Breena could never recognize. Her singing was soft, airy, like a light fall breeze blowing through your hair.

So, she sat as still as possible, watching the birds flitting from power line to power line and clutching her backpack to her like a lifeline. Her mother picked up speed as they drove down the road, taking them far, far away from their home. Looking back, she wished she had spent a little longer looking.

It felt like they drove for hours. Passing through towns Breena had never even heard of, until they reached the forest. Breena had never been this far away from town before, she had rarely even been outside her own house. Her mother didn't like her going outside. *You're delicate. Anything could just snatch you away from me if I'm not careful with you.*

Her mother was always worried about Breena vanishing into thin air, as if she'd fly away on the wind and never come back. She supposed she couldn't blame her mother for thinking like that. Whenever she sat, staring out the window, she would imagine herself as a bird soaring between the trees. She liked to imagine the joy that would come with a pair of wings, the freedom that would come with a pair of talons to rip into her prey. It must have been nice, being a bird.

The trees surrounding them grew denser and denser the further into the woods they drove. She could see the sun starting to peak over the horizon as they finally started to slow. There were a few driveways hidden amongst the dense foliage. The only way she noticed them was because of the brightly painted mailboxes near the street. They were painted different colors—baby blue, purple, firetruck red—and each had their own little design on them, from clouds to flowers to hand prints. They were really quite cute, and a nasty bug swirled in her gut. She wished she could have painted the mailbox with her mother. It would have been nice to do something together. She could imagine the paint splattered on her mother's cheek, the way she would smile as she looked over Breena's art.

But they never did any of that together, and though she didn't know it at the time, she never would.

Her mother took a sharp turn and drove down a long dirt path. The trees opened up and her mother parked the car in front of a lake. The rising sun painted the top of the too still water in swaths of glittering purple and orange. For a while, her mother kept her hands on the steering wheel, eyes staring straight out at the water. Her face was blank, devoid of any emotion. She didn't smile or pout. She just stared. Stared for so long that it started to scare Breena. *What was she thinking about? What was she looking at? What was she looking for?*

Her car door opened, and she stepped outside. The humid, summer air clung to her like a second skin, her hair frizzing up in the heat. Her mother shrugged off her cardigan and let it fall around her feet, leaving her in nothing but her long white dress as it billowed around her in a wind Breena couldn't feel. She bent to the ground and gathered stone after stone after stone and placed them in her pockets. This time though, her mother did not inspect the stone like she did with the seashells scattered around their house. Picked up a stone, put it away, picked up a stone, put it away, picked up, put away. Again and again, until her dress sagged with the weight of them.

When she finally stood back up, she turned to Breena and smiled. It was a wide, bright smile—all teeth and glittering eyes. She couldn't remember if her mother had ever smiled at her before. Breena pocketed the image, searing her mother's serene face into her mind. She felt her heart skip a beat and she wanted to run to her and throw her arms around her legs. She wanted to hold her, to slap her across the face, and pet her hair. She wanted to grab her mother by the shoulders and shake her, drag her back into the car. But before she could grab the door handle, her mother turned around again and waded into the water.

She walked until the water lapped against her chin and then, she was gone. As if she had never been standing there in the first place. Breena sat in the car, clutching her glittery backpack to her chest and waiting for her mother to come back, waiting for a ripple or a bubble to break the too still water. But the lake stayed still as glass and her mother never resurfaced.

It didn't take long for another car to pull up to the lake. A couple got out with their fishing poles but stopped as soon as they saw Breena sitting alone in the idling car, no mother or adult in sight.

The rest of the day was a blur of ambulances and policemen and cold plastic chairs. Until her grandmother came to pick her up. She hadn't known that it was her grandmother, at first. She hadn't known that she even had a grandmother.

There had been a letter in the glove box. It was meant to be a goodbye of sorts, but most of it had been a bunch of nonsensical rambling about the things that lived in the woods. Her handwriting barely legible. But her mother had left her grandmother's name and phone number at the bottom of the letter.

So that I won't be alone. That's what she told herself while she lay in bed staring into the dark, after she moved in with her grandmother, or Shannon, as she asked to be called. She didn't like being called grandma and Breena was just fine with that since she didn't like calling her grandma either.

She moved into her mother's old teenage bedroom, with bright yellow walls covered with old boy band posters, random drawings, old notes she had exchanged with friends behind the teacher's back in the middle of class. The bedspread was covered in little sunflowers and butterflies. Being in the room felt like standing in front of a looking glass. She could imagine her mother sitting at her desk and brushing her hair or putting on makeup while an old pop CD played in the speaker sitting on her bedside table. The thought of her mother laying in the same bed as her—at the same age as her—caused an uncomfortable tightness in Breena's chest.

Her mother, stoic and beautiful and savage, had once too been a young girl with bright eyes and a cheery smile. What happened? How could she so easily hug and kiss her friends in all these photographs scattered around her old room, but she could hardly bring herself to look Breena in the eye. Had she given away all her love? All her softness? Where did it go?

Overall, Shannon had a nice home—a little cottage at the edge of Devil's Pointe, full of crosses and pentagrams and iron horseshoes. The first thing Breena learned about her grandmother was that she was paranoid. She was constantly looking over her shoulder, always mumbling blessings under her breath, making the sign of the cross whenever she saw so much as a crow fly past the window. But she was the most paranoid about Breena. She didn't let her go to school or hang out with any of the other kids in town.

Breena couldn't complain too much though. Her grandmother always brushed her hair and gave her nice clothes. There was always food on the table and a book for her to read. Compared to the silent detonations of her mother, Shannon was a creature of spontaneity. She rarely did the same thing twice, whether it was a recipe or a route to town or the symphony of knocks she would perform to stop the pesky faeries from hearing them. She had dozens of shawls and bone necklaces and jangling bracelets that would adorn her body every day.

Shannon gave Breena all sorts of necklaces— rosaries with all different kinds of beads and colors, silver lockets, and simple iron crosses. She gave her wooden bracelets and rings, bundles of different flowers Breena could never remember the names of, and other innocent little trinkets. She spent hours brushing and braiding Breena's hair in intricate patterns. It was the only time they bonded. Shannon loved her hair.

Just like Breena had loved her mother's hair.

Things didn't get bad until a few years later.

Breena didn't remember much about what happened. She had a nightmare. A bad one. There was a baby in a crib that wouldn't stop crying. She had never been around a baby before, but she had seen all kinds of movies and shows with babies in them, so she wrapped it up in its blanket and held it close. She tried shushing it and bouncing it and rocking it, but nothing worked. It screamed and screamed and screamed until Breena could feel the tell-tale trickle of blood pouring out of her ears. But she just held the baby closer, tighter against her chest, until she felt a crack under her palm and the baby quieted.

She woke up in the woods, far from Shannon's house, standing in a clearing, full of blue and yellow flowers. There was a girl, just at the edge of the tree line watching her. Breena had never seen her before, with her long auburn hair and eyes that were too round for her face.

The girl waved, beckoning Breena closer to her, but Breena didn't dare move. The girl offered a wide smile, rows of sharp teeth glinting in the moonlight, her mouth and chin smeared red.

She was shaken awake. Shannon was screaming in her face to wake up and Breena found herself standing in that same clearing from her dream.

Just a dream, just a dream, just a dream.

But though she couldn't see her, Breena still felt the weight of the girl's gaze, buzzing at the crown of her head. As she came back to her senses and the edges of the dream faded away from her, she felt a warm stickiness covering her front, dripping from her chin to her nightgown. In her arms, was a limp, dead thing, soft and furry. A rabbit, she knew, though she couldn't bring herself to look at it. A defenseless, innocent rabbit. And she had killed it.

Blood. She was covered in blood. She could feel it gliding down her arms, matting in the poor thing's fur, on her tongue. Everywhere. It was everywhere. Tears pooled in her eyes, but not because she was sad. Her stomach yawned and begged and grew three sizes too big. She had to stop herself from lifting her fingers to her mouth and licking them clean.

Shannon kept shaking her and yelling. She was frantic, her eyes wild. She looked like a caged animal and Breena wondered just how much of her rage and her fear she was keeping locked away.

The feel of the rabbit's bones snapping and popping under the weight of her hold came back to her in a rush. She hadn't meant to hurt it, had only meant to cradle it gently like a mother might cradle her own child. Meant to care for it the way she had tried to care for her mother. Meant to be kind and soft and gentle, but her touch was too strong. She hadn't known when to ease up, hadn't known how to let it breathe.

It was an accident. It wasn't her fault. Couldn't be her fault.

By this point, Shannon had gotten ahold of herself. She stopped her shouting and only stared right through Breena as she ripped the bunny out of Breena's arms and ushered her by the shoulders back to the house. Breena kept her eyes trained on the rabbit's limp body, its stark white fur now dirtied and brown. She ruined it. Tainted it.

That night was the last time Breena slept in her bed freely. Shannon began keeping her shackled to the bedpost. The restraints, at least, were a soft leather, with a plush padding that sat against her wrists and ankles. It was only really a bother when she woke up in the middle of the night and had to go to the bathroom, but she managed it well enough.

The first time Breena saw Poppy was in her dream, though she had yet to meet her and couldn't have possibly known the girl in the trees was Poppy, but that didn't really matter. The second time was while waiting in line at the pharmacy for Shannon's prescription. Poppy was standing beside her father, small hands gripping so tightly onto her father's pants, Breena worried she might rip them. It was the moment Breena realized that Poppy was a real, tangible girl. It excited her, sent a little thrill up her spine.

But it was the third time Breena met her that she realized there was something deeply wrong with Poppy.

She had taken to standing outside Breena's bedroom window whenever Shannon was running errands in town. Poppy would wave at her and smile. It always felt like she was asking Breena to join her outside, but she never really did. She just smiled and waved and left. It irritated her, the way Poppy was free to come and go as she pleased.

After a year or so, Breena figured out that if she moved her wrists just right, she could slip out of the restraints Shannon kept her in. There was an end of the year party happening in the woods, far enough away from town that no one would know, and Breena decided to sneak out. Poppy had somehow snuck a note into her pocket without her noticing. She was always doing that—hiding bits and bobbles for Breena to find. A bone one day, a strip of fabric the next. It was always something small, something odd. It was always annoying.

But there had never been a note before. When Breena unfolded it, she expected some cryptic message about meeting under the next full moon or something weird like that. What she didn't expect was a party invite.

She had overheard some girls talking about it while walking through town and she would have been lying if she said she hadn't felt that stabbing pang of jealousy shoot through her abdomen as she watched the group of girls huddled together— sparkly nails dancing in the sun, giggles floating to her through the air. They had looked to be about her age. Probably went to the middle school with all of the other kids in town. All of the other kids, except Breena.

She wondered how different things would be if Shannon had let her go to school. Let her be around the kids her age. Let her join clubs or after-school activities. Let her be a kid. Let her be normal for once in her life.

It was the only thing she wanted. Friends. Companions. Someone to give all her love to. Someone to love her in return. She was so starved for it, ready to pounce on the first person to show her a lick of kindness and tear it out with her teeth.

She hadn't expected the invite, hadn't even expected Poppy to be invited. It was no secret that girls like Breena were able to mostly fly under the radar because of Poppy. She was the town's resident psycho.

Breena thought about the invite and Poppy and the party while she pretended to get ready for bed that night. She brushed her teeth, knelt at the altar Shannon had made for an hour pretending to pray, let Shannon shackle her to the bed, and waited until the house fell still. Shannon was a light sleeper, but her room was far away enough from Breena's that she didn't hear her getting dressed or grabbing the camera she found in the lost and found by the old gas station off the highway, or the window opening and closing. She didn't hear the soft thump of Breena's sneakers hitting the dewy grass, before she took off into the forest.

She followed the faint drone of whispered voices and distant music, the trees closing in on her the further she walked away from her home. The night was so warm it was almost sticky, but Breena clutched her flannel in her shaking hands. Her shoulder hurt, pain radiating from the now burned skin. It was a rune of some kind. Breena didn't know what it meant but it was supposed to keep the supposed demons out of her body, at least according to Shannon it was.

Most of the scars were on her back, some dotted her arms, and a few had ended up on her leg. They were all different symbols or runes from different religions and beliefs. It didn't matter where they came from as long as they kept the bad away. It hurt, but it made Shannon happy, made her feel secure, so Breena didn't complain. She took a handful of painkillers before she left, and though her head swam whenever she walked too fast or moved too suddenly, it did help.

It didn't take long for Breena to learn that the forest in Devil's Pointe had a bad reputation—buried under stories of young girls vanishing into thin air and boys being eaten. She didn't really believe the stories at first, and up until her sleepwalking incident, she had been under the impression that Devil's Pointe was still just operating on old 1600s Puritan beliefs. Beliefs that imaginary monsters and devils trying to drag your soul to hell lived in the darkness.

But the sleepwalking—the dream. That had been real. The rabbit had been real.

Poppy had been real.

Breena once thought that it might be nice to meet whatever beast was hiding in the shadows, but now that Poppy found her in dreams, Breena didn't hold that sentiment anymore. Shannon believed that dreams held meaning and that certain demons could take hold of your mind while you were sleeping, while you were vulnerable and silent. Demons that stole your breath and invaded your thoughts.

As her boots padded against the soft grass and mud, she wondered if Poppy was hiding somewhere, watching her. She hadn't felt the tell-tale tingle buzzing under her skin that usually happened when Poppy's gaze traveled along her body.

The warmth from the bonfire hit her face before she noticed the noise. Music was blaring from a CD player at the other end of the clearing and kids were all crowded around a punch bowl filled to the brim with a fluorescent pink liquid that would no doubt taste like something akin to battery acid. Some kids were drinking or smoking, others were dancing, fewer were separating from the group in pairs.

It seemed odd, for kids so young to rebel in the mature ways they did. Some blamed it on the lack of parental supervision, most blamed it on the influence of the Devil, but the problem—the real problem—was that there wasn't anything to do in Devil's Pointe. The nearest gas station was a 20-minute bike ride outside of town. There wasn't a mall or shopping center or big-name superstore that didn't take over an hour to drive to. Getting drunk and stealing cigarettes from behind the corner store counter while the cashier wasn't looking was the most exciting thing anyone could do in this town.

As Breena scanned the crowd, she realized that Poppy was nowhere to be seen, but that didn't stop the hairs at the back of her neck from standing up. Didn't stop the way her breath quickened, and her heart stuttered. Just because Breena couldn't see her, didn't mean that she wasn't here. Poppy was always there like some first-rate creeper.

She recognized most of the kids from around town, but there was one girl that Breena hadn't immediately recognized. There were whispers of a new girl that had managed to lay low, until now. Vivien sat on an old tree stump, her black stocking clad legs swinging back and forth beneath her as an older boy sat next to her. He whispered something in her ear that made her giggle while he threaded her long dark hair through his fingers. His other hand rested on her knee, toying with the edge of her long, red plaid skirt.

But she wasn't interested in him. For a moment, Vivien's eyes locked with Breena's, and she shot her a small smirk before lifting her cup to her mouth.

She hadn't been able to stop herself from taking a picture of

Vivien as her head tilted back and she pretended to laugh at some joke the boy told her. The picture was dark and a bit out of focus, but Vivien still glowed in the light of the fire. It was the first picture she ever took, a picture she would keep with her and add to in later years.

Breena walked over to the bowl of punch and grabbed herself a cup. Nobody looked at her for too long, not like they did when she was walking through town with Shannon and suddenly, she wondered if the sneers and whispers were never even meant for her. Maybe the hatred she felt directed at her from the people of Devil's Pointe was imagined.

Here, she was almost invisible. It was a feeling she liked more than she had ever imagined she would.

She took a sip from her cup, nearly retching as a scent reminiscent of isopropyl alcohol filled her nostrils. The taste wasn't much better. It was sweet the way a handful of skittles was sweet, but it burned so badly she nearly coughed.

Breena watched as Vivien hopped off her stump, leaving the boy behind without a second glance, and joined a group of kids about to play spin the bottle. She smiled and nodded her head, beckoning Breena over. Who was she to reject such an invitation?

She didn't know much about Vivien besides the fact that she didn't live with her father. She was pretty with a soft, full mouth and delicate hands, and she seemed so confident. Her lips didn't curl in disgust whenever she took a sip of her drink, her gaze didn't waver as she looked up at the boy still talking to her, she didn't flinch away when his hand traveled from her knee to her thigh. Breena wanted to be like that.

Sitting down in the slightly damp grass a few bodies away from Vivien, Breena knotted her fingers together. It felt so odd, to be so near kids her own age and not feel their mocking stares. It would make sense, she supposed, that the meaner, uptight kids weren't privy to the late-night parties. Breena couldn't help but smile at the thought.

For a while, Breena did nothing but sit and watch. The bottle spun and spun and spun and boys and girls and girls and girls and boys and boys kissed cheeks and hands and noses and lips. She watched as Vivien sat back and drank from her cup each time the bottle landed on her to avoid kissing anyone.

There was a nudge on her shoulder and the bottle was pushed towards her so she could reach. She hadn't realized anyone noticed she was there, and it sent an odd prickling through her chest. Vivien watched her with her eyes, so dark they seemed bottomless in the soft night glow of the bonfire. Breena liked when Vivien watched her. There was never any judgment in her gaze, only assessment, curiosity. Vivien made her feel like a subject worthy of study.

Breena got up onto her knees and spun the bottle, watching as it turned and turned and turned until it finally landed on a boy with sandy, mussed hair and soft green eyes. He had the kind of face that would end up on a boy band poster with his pretty cheekbones and soft eyes. Sometimes Breena would see him working at the corner store with his dad and sometimes she would go in to buy a pack of gum or a candy bar just so she could see him.

He smiled at her and rose up to meet her halfway. His smile was her undoing. She wasn't used to smiles, but somehow, she knew his was particularly melty. Glancing down at the cup in her hand, she set it down on the ground. She could have taken a sip, like Vivien and a few other girls had whenever they didn't want to kiss whoever the bottle landed on.

But Breena wanted to kiss him. So, she raised herself on her knees and shuffled towards him, her hands landing on his shoulders with a soft thud. Her breath caught in her throat as he lowered his face to hers. She curled her fingers into his white t-shirt as their mouths met. It was uncoordinated and awkward in the way that all first kisses are. There was too much teeth and spit but it sent a buzz spreading under her skin nonetheless. The way his hands held her waist in a vice-like grip felt holy. The way his heart thumped against her hand felt divine. She couldn't remember the last time she had been this close to anyone. Her mother, perhaps? A year or two before her demise? Breena certainly didn't know, and at the moment, she hadn't cared at all.

All she cared about was the feeling of his heartbeat under her palms, the way she could practically feel the way his blood moved beneath his skin, and the way his skin tasted so tart, like lemon pie. She imagined biting into his lip, hard enough to draw blood. Imagined the feel of his skin between her teeth. She hadn't wanted to hurt him. She hadn't known exactly what she wanted. All she knew was that her head throbbed and she was hungry, empty.

She didn't care much for the kiss itself, exactly, only for the way his soft hands felt on her and the way his breath ghosted over her face. He held her in the same way one might hold a baby bird with a broken wing. Or he did, until she tried pulling away.

The moment their mouths separated, his fingers dug into her shirt, and he kissed her harder, demanding more and more and more until her lips went numb from the pressure. At some point, she registered that he was biting her lower lip so hard blood was pooling down her chin and staining her tank top.

She remembered making some gurgling sound of panic and shoving her hands against his chest, but he wouldn't budge. Her blood slicked between the two of their faces.

He just grabbed her harder, bringing her closer to him as if he would die without her body pressed to his. She tried kicking him and hitting him, but nothing worked. Vivien was the one to push him to the ground. She even managed to get in a few punches and kicks to the groin before he registered what happened. His pupils were blown wide, his cheeks flushed, and if Breena hadn't known any better, she would have thought he snarled at her. His breathing was ragged and loud, and Breena could've sworn she could see the harsh thumping of his heart from inside his chest.

Breena fell to the grass, hands clutching her mouth when a pair of hands dragged her back up and quickly ushered her away.

Poppy led Breena through the woods, the sounds of the party dissipating the further they walked. If she were in less pain, Breena liked to think she would have argued, would have pushed Poppy away and found some cold, dark corner to bandage herself. But she let Poppy lead her through the trees until they came to a small creek, the water babbling in the dark the only source of noise. The night was still as a corpse. There was no wind blowing through the trees, no animals rustling in the underbrush—just the soft squelch of Breena's shoes moving over the muddy ground.

Poppy sat Breena down by the creek, "Keep pressure on it. It'll hurt but it won't be for long."

Breena kept her flannel sleeve pressed against her mouth, the bite marks now hot to the touch as the pain seared through her chin and jaw. If he had held on any longer, he could have sliced her lip clean off. A part of her feared he may have.

Poppy returned a moment later, her hands smeared black with what Breena could only assume was mud from the creek. Shannon often told her about mud and the way the rivers and lakes and streams and creeks in Devil's Pointe could heal you of any ailment. But they were always so deep in the woods that Shannon didn't trust them anymore. The evil of the woods trumped the purity of the water. Poppy clearly didn't think that way.

"Move your hands now. It's fine. It'll be fine. People like us heal quickly. The mud is only meant to help soothe the pain." Poppy's voice was softer than Breena expected. It had a melodic, almost honeyed, quality to it. She pronounced her syllables slow, elongating her vowels and smoothing over the harsh consonants.

Breena hadn't been scared of her in the dream, hadn't been scared when she was just a dream. But in the daylight, Breena couldn't pretend Poppy wasn't real. She was too real. Their faces were inches apart, centimeters even, and Breena was surrounded by Poppy's sweet earthy scent—something akin to amber or moss. This close, she couldn't stop herself from imagining what it would have been like to kiss Poppy instead of that boy. She might have enjoyed it more. Might not have ended the night covered in her own blood.

Poppy's fingers gently moved Breena's hands away from her mouth and ghosted over the bite; Breena's heart ran wild in her chest. The boy had managed to bite through her lip, but only partly. Breena couldn't stop her tongue from running over the injury. She wouldn't admit to herself until much later that the impulse came from some well buried part of her that liked the smooth metallic taste of her own blood running down her throat.

Poppy smeared the mud on Breena's injury, taking extra care to not press too hard. "Boys can't handle themselves around us. It isn't our fault. We give them a kind word, a smile, a wave..." she hesitated, "a kiss and they go wild. They're incapable of control. They're like animals that have been locked in a cage without food for too long."

Breena focused on Poppy's delicate eyebrows—a few shades darker than her chocolate brown hair. The mud smelled of freshwater fish and algae, but it was a welcoming scent compared to the overwhelming smell of Poppy.

"But that's what they never realize. They aren't the animals. They just like to pretend they are. It's us who have been in cages. Us who are the animals. Us who are hungry." Poppy stared at Breena for a long time, almost waiting to see if she would run away. Breena stayed sitting in the grass, her hands digging into the earth beneath her. "I'm sure Vivien taught him a lesson. She's good at that. Defending her own. That's why I like her so much."

"Why do you like me?" The question spilled from Breena's lips like rocks tumbling down a hill in an avalanche.

Poppy shrugged, wiping her dirtied hands over her skirt. The white fabric now stained dark with a mixture of Breena's blood and creek mud. "The same reasons. You seem like the scrappy type. I can almost smell it on you. You just haven't had the chance to prove it yet. But you will. Trust me."

Breena almost smiled at the thought of being the reason for Poppy's disorderly appearance. After Breena's lip stopped bleeding and the earthy taste of the mud coated her tongue, Poppy stood up, preparing to walk away without another word. As Breena opened her mouth to thank her, Poppy held a finger up to her mouth and shook her head. "Don't thank me. It's bad luck." She winked at her, before turning on her heel and walking off into the darkness.

By the time Breena snuck back in through her window and silently washed the mud from her face, the bite dulled to a mere mark on her skin. One that would be gone before morning.

Breena - Present

After a long silent walk, Breena and Jamie broke through the trees and came upon the Farm. It was far less menacing in the daylight, but that didn't stop the goose flesh that ran up her arms or the shiver that ran down her spine. She felt like a lit match sitting too close to a gas can.

"So, this is the famous Farm?" Jamie asked. He trained his camera on the scenery around them and focused the shot. Unlike other campsites, the Farm didn't have any signs or fence posts advertising itself. There was only a gate and an archway at the entrance, now rusted and falling apart. The girls used to say it was a portal to hell. Once you came in, you never came out. The Farm was a hellmouth that ate and ate and ate and never stopped.

It was still eating, still hungry, even in its ruin.

Breena pointedly ignored him and walked them towards the mess hall—feeling too exposed just standing in the middle of the semi-empty courtyard. All the plants had withered away, and the grass was now a burnt yellow that crunched under every step the pair took. At one point in time, it had been filled with games, picnic tables, a makeshift tennis court, and even a small garden. None of it had ever really been for them. It was mainly for show, but sometimes if the wardens were in a good mood, the girls could convince them to let them play a game or two while the Freels were away.

Satisfaction crawled its way up her body before she could stamp it down. Breena enjoyed looking at the sad little shell this place that was once so full of horror and fear had become. Years of neglect and abandonment had left the Farm dilapidated. Most of the cabins that the girls had slept in were intact, but windows were broken, and doors were hanging off hinges. The mess hall was the worst building by far. The roof had almost entirely caved in on itself. Broken wooden planks were scattered throughout the grass as if a storm had torn a path through the camp and bits of broken glass were blown about in the wind.

"What happened?" Jamie asked, "I thought it had only been a few years since the Farm was shut down?"

"The weather." Breena shoved her hands into her coat pockets.

Jamie chuckled, but when he didn't respond, Breena sighed and offered, "The spring after Poppy disappeared it pretty much never stopped raining, but the wood had been rotting long before that. It was just a matter of time before one bad storm came along and blew it all away."

The inside of the mess hall was just as bad as the outside. Vines and weeds had overtaken the walls and lunch tables. Cracks had formed in the foundation where weeds had begun growing through. The weak sunlight filtered through the dusty windows, casting the large room in a hazy glow that reminded Breena of the old stained-glass windows in the Freels church. She hadn't been inside the church a lot but sometimes, when Shannon was feeling extra confrontational, she'd take Breena along with her and she'd get to sit in an empty pew and stare up at the statue of Jesus on the Cross.

If she were anyone else, she might find the mess hall to be beautiful. There was something growing and thriving in the chaos that had been left behind. Something was surviving off the rot and pollution of what was left of the Farm. The weeds and vines and grass were reclaiming what rightfully belonged to them. It was poetic and, in another life, she might have liked to photograph it.

Breena once considered doing an installation about the Farm, but she couldn't bring herself to document it—iconize it. It didn't deserve that. Her attention, the world's attention. No matter how terrible it looked in the daylight. She wanted the place to be completely forgotten, written over. They all did. Aislin never painted it. Vivien never wrote about it. Breena tried her hardest not to think about it.

But it wasn't enough. It was never enough. She wanted to take an axe to every wall that remained standing, every window that remained unbroken and smash it all to hell. She wanted it destroyed. Utterly decimated.

The same way it had left her.

And Aislin.

And Vivien.

And Poppy.

Jamie walked over a pile of broken glass, startling Breena out of her thoughts. It was easy to get lost in the ghosts of the memories that still lived there.

"So, if you don't care about Poppy, what do you want to know?" Breena still wasn't sure she truly believed he meant what he said. But he seemed so honest, as if it wouldn't make any sense for him to lie.

"Obviously I *have* to care about Poppy. She started it all. But

I want to know about you. I mean, you guys are some of the most hated girls in America. Second only to Casey Anthony or Ted Bundy. You have to have some feelings about that."

"Do you know why?" Breena asked, finally looking up at Jamie. Vivien wanted them to talk to Jamie. Aislin did it. So why couldn't Breena?

That didn't mean she was going to be nice about it.

"Why what?"

"Why they hate us?" Her eyes grew cold, darkening with some far away fire that made him flinch. She reveled in that flash of fear that sparked through his eyes, "Well, do you?"

He merely shook his head and went back to fiddling with his camera.

"When people like you make a documentary or write a book inserting yourself into a tragedy where you don't belong, you're praised—labeled creative visionaries or artists. And when you make hundreds of thousands of dollars by ripping out the stitches of an unhealed wound, no one bats an eye. But when we try to move on, try to take our pain and put it into something that isn't ourselves, we become callous monsters. We're cruel, insensitive girls. But all girls are cruel and insensitive. The difference between us is that we went into those woods. We had to claw our way out. And it was us that had to wake up in the mud and realize that our best friend didn't come out with us."

Breena let out a long breath.

"That's a lot of weight to bear."

Breena let out a humorless chuckle and rolled her eyes, "Tell me about it. We were 16. Girls our age were planning dates and shopping. Even before that we never just got to be—"

But somehow, Jamie knew enough to understand. "Just kids?"

Breena nodded.

"My older sister went missing when I was only five. I get what it's like to grow up too fast."

Jamie's missing older sister was news to her. She had to admit that she hadn't cared enough to do any research on him. Did Vivien know? Is that why she was so okay with him interviewing them? Is that why he was so interested in having them be the stars of his next film?

She recognized it for what it was—an olive branch.

He said nothing as he fiddled with his camera.

"Right after I broke out into the photography scene, I shot this collection inspired by all the bullshit that happened to land us here," Breena waved a hand at their surroundings, taking a seat at one of the only lunch tables that hadn't completely fallen apart. "You should've seen the uproar. Or maybe you already have. I don't know. People hated it. They thought it was outrageous, disgusting, improper. There was even a petition to have my showcase canceled. But do you think I struggled to sell any of the photos? Do you think I struggled to sell any tickets to its opening night? Of course not. The tickets sold so fast the site crashed and every photograph had been purchased before the doors even opened."

"What did happen to land all of you here? This place is—"

"Creepy as shit?" Breena picked a dandelion from the ground and twirled it between her fingers. She didn't like recounting the incident. The humiliation. The fear. But she doubted anyone would see this footage anyways.

"We were all about fifteen, just before the start of sophomore year, and we had gone to the traveling carnival that came to Devil's Pointe every summer. It was a sort of last hurrah before school or whatever. Kids snuck in all kinds of alcohol and drugs and what have you. Anything to keep the night entertaining." The yearly summer carnival was just about the only fun thing that ever came to Devil's Pointe—or came around Devil's Pointe. The carnival actually stopped a town over, but it was a Devil's Pointe staple, nonetheless.

If she closed her eyes, she could still feel the heat of the fluorescent lights from the rides on her face, still taste the cotton candy Aislin had shared with her, still smell Vivien's perfume, still hear Poppy's laugh.

"There was this boy. He was a bit older, and we had kissed during a stupid game of spin the bottle back in middle school, though I can't remember his name now. He spent the entire night at the carnival following us around with a few of his friends. He did that a lot. Followed me around everywhere. Aislin thought it was kind of sweet, but the rest of us kept making fun of him. We thought he was like a lovesick puppy, but I guess I was just thankful that he wasn't as aggressive as some of the other kids in our school."

Poppy had been right that night by the river all those years ago. All it took was a look, a smile, and people became crazed. Spin the bottle boy had only been her first lesson, and second, but he certainly wasn't her last.

"It wasn't until the fireworks ended that he had come over and asked me on a date. I don't know why I said yes. It was stupid, but I just wanted to be a normal kid for one night. So when the day rolled around, I told Shannon, my grandmother, that I was spending the night with Poppy. The Freels were the only family in Devil's Pointe Shannon respected so Poppy was always my cover. She didn't like me hanging out with the neighborhood kids. Hell, she barely tolerated Poppy."

"Why? From the way Aislin spoke it sounded like everyone

in Devil's Pointe was religious."

"Please, Shannon wasn't just religious. She was a zealot—a borderline doomsday cultist—and she didn't think the rest of the town took it all seriously enough. She was intense and the Freels always enabled her. They were a lot scarier behind closed doors." Breena knew all too well how horrifying the Freels were. Poppy told them everything and in turn, they told her everything. They laid out the darkest parts of themselves to be feasted upon as their nightly ritual. "That's one of the reasons we all got along so well. Our families were psychotic."

She remembered the meetings over tea and sandwiches, the closed doors in the back of the church, the whispered conversations about exorcisms and demonic possession. Shannon had always been extreme, and Breena had waited for the day the Freels would talk some kind of sense into her. But they never did. They were parasitic. Feeding off of one another's delusions and growing sicker together with each passing day.

"Poppy tried talking me out of going on the date, but I wouldn't listen to her. I just wanted to have fun—go out with a cute boy, turn my brain off for a night. Vivien may have been uneasy, but she hadn't said anything, just helped Aislin get me ready. They did my hair and my makeup while Poppy picked out my outfit. It was the first time I felt like a regular kid."

It was so relaxing to just be a teenager for once. To not think about Shannon and her deranged rituals. The brands on her back. Her dead mother.

"When I met the kid at the carnival for the date, I was buzzing. It was the last night it would be in town, so we went all out. He bought me cotton candy and tickets so we could go on all the rides. We played all the games, and we had this bet that whoever won the most got to keep all the prizes."

"None of that sounds very Farm worthy? I can't imagine sneaking out once was enough to do you in."

Breena's smile faded as she thought back to that night. A worm wiggled in the dirt by her boot. A bird landed on the roof, peering down at the two of them as they spoke.

"When the fireworks ended, we dropped all the prizes off in the backseat of his car, and we started to drive back to the Freels. He ended up pulling off to the side of the road—it was all dark and wooded—and he started kissing me. It was the second time we kissed, my second time kissing anyone."

Aislin had given all the girls bundles of yarrow to carry around to protect them. She was always carrying those weird flowers in her pockets, tucked into her tube socks. Though the flowers always gave her a throbbing headache, it kept the craziness that followed them at bay.

But that night, the flowers hadn't worked to keep the craziness from boiling inside Breena. The boy had surprisingly been respectful: kept his hands above her waist or at the back of her neck and didn't force her closer to him than necessary. But the moment Breena's lips touched his, a frenzy started. In that car, she finally understood how he had felt during that stupid game of spin-the-bottle. She tasted his skin and couldn't stop herself from imagining how his ribs would feel snapping between her fingers, how his blood would feel sliding down her throat.

"Did you not want to kiss him?"

Breena shook her head, "No, I mean I definitely did. A lot."

"There's nothing wrong with that. You grew up in a religious household, so it makes sense that the shame and guilt crept up on you."

"It wasn't just that though," Breena said, rolling her eyes. "I didn't just want to kiss him I—"

The sun steadily rose over their heads, but the clouds seemed to only grow denser.

"Wanted to eat him?"

Breena's eyes snapped to Jamie's, "What the hell are you talking about?"

Spring formal. Bethany.

Her shoulder.

The bite that had been taken out of her shoulder.

Jamie put his hands up in mock surrender, "It's ok. I'm not judging."

"Oh, fuck off. Where are you getting this from?"

"Every good interviewer has their sources," he said. "This is your story. You get to choose how it gets told. We can roll the footage and pick up where we left off, or we can pretend I hadn't asked you that. It's your choice."

"We aren't cannibals," Breena said, her eyes falling to the ground. Her voice had gone up a pitch. She didn't need to explain herself to him. He wasn't worth defending herself to, and yet, she still felt that innately human urge to seem *normal*.

"I didn't say you were."

"It's just something in us that we can't control. We spend so much of our time keeping it in check, staying in line, keeping it caged. But when he kissed me, it just came over me. Like it flipped a switch. I was too hot and too distracted. My stomach hurt so badly, as if someone had reached inside me and twisted it with their hands. I bit his neck so hard he started bleeding, but I stopped myself before it got too bad. All I could think about was ripping him open. What his bone marrow would taste like. How soft his liver would be." Breena let out a dry chuckle, "I ended up running out of his car into the middle of the woods. I could hear him yelling at me to come back. To *finish what I started."*

A spider fell on her jacket covered arm. Despite the afternoon sun, the air was getting colder. The wind picked up, blowing a few stray strands of hair into her face. She didn't bother to push them away.

"It started raining but I hadn't even noticed. I was just so focused on not hurting anything. There was still some of his blood on my tongue and every lick sent a zap down my spine. I thought I was going crazy. I hadn't ever felt like that before. So utterly consumed with the thought of eating another person. Somehow, I made it back to Poppy's house. Her parents had gone out for the night, some midnight Bible group for the town insomniacs. When Poppy opened the door, I was soaked to the bone. Even after the girls got me out of the shower and dressed, I was shaking so hard you could hear my teeth chattering all the way downstairs."

Aislin had started crying while toweling Breena off in the foyer, while Poppy was trying to convince Vivien to not beat the shit out of spin the bottle boy.

She hadn't been able to stop the events of the night from falling out of her mouth like water over a cliff. She remembered that she had been so hungry and the pain in her stomach only kept getting worse. Even now, that same feeling crept up her spine and settled at the base of her neck.

"By the time I told them everything I was half-delirious. I couldn't think straight. But then Poppy had this idea. And Vivien agreed with her. Apparently, the two of them had talked about it before. Vivien had been the first of us to deal with the *cravings*—that's what she called them." Everything for Vivien had happened first. But that was her story to tell, not Breena's.

"Poppy's dad liked to hunt with some of the other older men

in the congregation and he had brought back some deer or rabbit or whatever from their latest hunting trip. Poppy and Viv grabbed it out of the fridge and laid it out in front of Aislin and me like some pseudo-last supper. It was raw and bloody, and it was one of the best things I had ever tasted. At the time."

They had circled around the plate of raw meat on the floor and devoured it together.

Breena pretended it was the boy's insides she was scooping into her mouth. Pretended it was the boy's blood that was trickling down her chin.

She imagined the other girls were playing pretend just like she was.

"Poppy said we were different. Special. I just hadn't realized she was being so literal."

Jamie stepped towards her, "Did someone catch you?"

"Obviously." Breena sighed. "The jackass apparently followed me out of the car and caught up with me at Poppy's. He must have been pissed that I ran off because the next day our lockers were smeared in fake blood. Someone even took the time to kindly spray paint "slut" on mine. Kids called us cannibals as they passed us in the hallways. No one would go anywhere near us. They all thought we were either completely psychotic, or demon possessed. So, the Freels stepped in and sent us off to the Farm."

Vivien - Present

Rarer yet, the story started with Vivien Cullen, but it often liked to end with her. Vivien had been the last girl to embrace Poppy, but she had been the easiest to convince. She thought about Poppy as she stood at the living room window and watched Breena walk back up the long driveway with Jamie in tow. Breena had fought with her about doing the documentary, but Vivien had managed to convince her. There were no secrets between the girls. They shared everything with one another. But there were so many things between them that they left unspoken. Things they all knew and felt, but never dared utter out loud. They didn't always need to put their feelings into words, but she thought they needed to start trying.

Vivien knew better than any of them how important words were. Aislin and Breena preferred the visual mediums of painting and photography, but Vivien wrote and wrote and wrote, finding solace in the way she could paint an imaginary image directly into someone's head with a poem, a word.

Poppy preferred the art of keeping secrets and, in turn, the rest of them had followed suit. Despite the years they've spent attached at the hip, there was still so much they needed to say, to understand. Aislin and Breena were so skittish. The night Breena came to them after her first date, she and Aislin had almost thrown up with nervous excitement at the mere suggestion of eating raw meat.

It was merely the first steppingstone to something more, and it most certainly wasn't the last.

They had gotten over the meat, but not the act. It still made them squirm like worms washed up on the sidewalk after a storm. They'd get over it soon though.

Aislin eventually sided with Vivien after some nudging, but Breena continued to fight with her the entire drive up to the cabin. She was angry and raging. Though Poppy brought them together, it was Breena that protected them like a mother wolf with its cubs. Their trips up to the cabin were sacred, secret. The girls were sacred, secret and Vivien couldn't blame Breena for feeling that way.

The entire night prior, Vivien had lied awake wondering whether bringing Jamie to the cabin was a good idea. But the moment she saw Breena walking back to the cabin with Jamie, her shoulders back and her face lifting towards the sunlight, Vivien realized she had made the right choice.

Breena had spent the entire morning at the Farm with Jamie and now the mid-afternoon sun was boiling high. Vivien recalled the way she would sit in the kitchen watching Poppy cook while Aislin sat on one of the barstools sketching the scene and Breena sat in the bay window. Poppy had always been the best cook out of all of them. She knew how to bake the sweetest desserts and the most decadent meals. Mrs. Freel had never liked cooking, and Pastor Freel thought it was the woman's job to serve dinner, so Poppy had been the one to take up the mantel.

The rest of them shied away from food at first. Aislin would sneak bites out of a protein bar, Breena would eat slices of plain bread or a bagel, while Vivien tended to avoid eating at all.

Nothing satisfied them.

But once they started coming to the cabin, things quickly changed. They would go through boxes of pizza rolls, shovel cereal into their mouths, empty boxes of ice cream, eat all the chips, Pop Tarts, cookies—anything the girls could get their hands on, they ate—until the kitchen was empty. But the more they ate, the hungrier they became. Poppy would make soup and meat and noodles, anything she could scrounge together with the few ingredients the teenage girls were able to get their hands on at the grocery store, but nothing worked.

They had spent so long being hungry that they found very few things could satiate their ever-empty stomachs. No matter how much they ate, the pit inside them never left. It had started slowly, minor hunger pains between meals, until the hunger grew and grew and grew before they could no longer take it.

Vivien walked to the front door to meet them on the porch and smiled, "Is it my turn in front of the camera now?"

Breena let out a humorless chuckle, "Knock your socks off. I never want to do this again."

Jamie shook his head at her and fiddled with his camera settings as he climbed up the porch steps, "It wasn't that bad. Let me just upload the footage I got, and we'll be good to go."

He walked inside and disappeared into the guest room as if he owned the place. Breena rolled her eyes and grabbed Vivien's hand. She was never good at asking for physical comfort, none of them ever were. They got used to just taking it when they needed it, and it worked for them.

"How did it go?" Vivien wrapped her arms around Breena's shoulders from behind and walked them towards the couch.

"We know that he knows," Aislin said as took the seat beside Breena, picking at the skin around her fingernails. "Did you talk to him about *it*?"

Vivien knew that Jamie knew *something*, but she hadn't been able to quite figure out what exactly it was that he found out about them. She sighed at Aislin's use of the word "it." Hopefully, once the night came, Aislin would be less apprehensive.

"Did he talk to someone from town? We all know that those *rumors* followed us all the way to Farm." Breena crossed her arms over her chest and leaned her head against the back of the couch.

"You know as well as I do how tight-lipped Devil's Pointe is. Not even Bethany would have talked to him. Besides," Vivien said, "They're all terrified of us. They all still think we're demonically possessed and would damn their souls to hell if they said anything about us to an *outsider*."

"I guess it doesn't matter. It's not like anyone else will find out." Aislin sighed, still picking at a hangnail on her thumb. Vivien settled her hand over Aislin's to get her to stop.

Aislin's words hung in the air around them and settled around their shoulders like a soft blanket.

"We should get the bonfire started. I need something to do," Breena said as she stood up and walked out the back door.

Vivien stood up and stretched her legs, "You go help. I'll finish dinner. I know how you loathe cooking."

Aislin laughed and pressed a kiss to Vivien's shoulder before running off to find Breena.

Vivien went to the kitchen and resumed cutting up the vegetables that Aislin had left out. When the sun started to dip and she heard the quiet opening and closing of the guest room door, Jamie ushered himself into the kitchen and sat in the bay window. She watched over her shoulder as he turned the camera on and angled it the way he needed.

"What are you making?"

Vivien turned back to the pot on the stove, "Vegetable soup. It was Poppy's favorite; she'd add all kinds of herbs and mushrooms from the forest outside. Taught us how to find them ourselves. The first time we spent the night up here alone Poppy taught us how to make it and now we have it every year we come up. It's a simple recipe, so I hope you like it."

"I'm not a very picky eater." Jamie laughed. "How did Poppy learn about all those ingredients?"

"Pastor Freel was an avid hunter. He'd come up every year during hunting season and teach Poppy all about living off the land. Mrs. Freel started a garden out back though after Poppy accidentally ate a berry that made her sick. But the Freels don't come up here anymore, so it's always empty for us this time of year."

"You guys come up here as a sort of yearly memorial, right?"

Vivien nodded, "Today's the anniversary of the day we all went missing, but I'm sure you already knew that. We don't do anything particularly special. It's simple, but when the three of us are together up here, it's like she's still with us."

"What do you guys do?"

Vivien turned towards the window and pointed outside with the knife in her hand. If she let her mind slip, she could mistake her hand for her father's. She stamped down the shudder that tried to fight its way through her body at the memory and focused her attention back on Jamie.

"We start a bonfire and spend the night around it. None of us really liked fire when we were younger—some weird irrational fear we all shared—but Poppy managed to convince us that we needed to overcome it."

"You're all scared of fire?"

"We were. There was a fire at the church during one of the Sunday services. The whole town was there, and we got locked in. The doors got stuck or the locks jammed, either way we couldn't get out. The building was rotting and rusted so it was only a matter of time before something like that happened. Luckily, it didn't spread too much before Pastor Freel and a few other men put it out. Everyone was convinced we had started it."

"Did you? Start the fire?"

Vivien dumped the cooked vegetables and spices into the boiling broth. "No, we didn't. But no one believed us anyways, so it doesn't really matter if we did or not."

"It seems like you guys got accused of a lot of things when you were young."

"We were easy targets. It was easier to believe that the four girls who spent all their time together whispering and running in the woods were the troublemakers. One of the altar boys knocked over a candle in the back while the four of us were sitting in the service. But we were still the ones who were blamed for it. It was expected of us to misbehave."

"How often did you guys ever actually misbehave?"

She stirred the soup clockwise three times, before covering it and leaning her back against the counter to face him. "Not often. Sometimes we'd sneak out into the woods after curfew, but that was it. There were all these stories of devils living in the woods waiting to eat children and steal their souls. It was all very Puritan, and I guess that was enough to convince the town of our evil doings with the devil."

"What would you guys do in the woods?"

Vivien smiled to herself, "We used to play pretend. Re-enacting fairy tales and the like. Aislin was always Cinderella, Breena was Rapunzel, and Poppy was Snow White. We'd combine our stories and hunt the wolf or rescue the princes from their towers, swim with mermaids at the river and climb the trees with faeries." They loved faeries. From Tinkerbell and Thumbelina to Maleficent and Morgan le Fay, they devoured fairy tales and mythology until their eyes burned and heads ached. "We felt hunted, ostracized, cast out into exile—such a common fairy tale trope that we couldn't help but see ourselves in them. We were determined to make it through, just like every heroine in every book we read. We hated unhappy endings."

"Which fairy tale were you?"

Vivien smiled, "The Maiden Without Hands."

Jamie grimaced. "Well, that's a bit harrowing."

"You know it? It isn't very popular, but I loved it. I always thought of Poppy as my angel in the garden, guiding me to the fruit tree so I wouldn't starve."

"My sister loved fairy tales. The creepier the better."

Vivien's ears pricked at the mention of his sister, "Was your movie about her? The one you got all those awards for. I watched it. It was a nasty piece of work, but I thoroughly enjoyed it. Aislin couldn't stomach it though and Breena didn't want to give you the time of day."

Jamie shifted in his seat, his eyes narrowed, "I didn't know you researched me."

She shrugged before turning back to the stove and stirring the soup, "I wasn't just going to invite a random person I knew nothing about up to this cabin with us. Imagine how stupid that would be. You still didn't answer my question, though."

Vivien knew the answer in the way he avoided her eyes. The girl in the movie was older than his sister, sure, but she couldn't ignore the glaringly obvious similarities. The sick baby renewed overnight, the raw meat, the faerie music, the hill.

His sister's *kidnapping* had followed a slew of animal mutilations in his town, and if anyone put the pieces together, they'd realize it mirrored Poppy's own story. The dead animals just hadn't been mentioned to anyone outside of Devil's Pointe. Most people had thought it was the work of a budding serial killer.

Vivien wasn't most people.

Jamie tensed, turning to look behind him out the window. For a moment, he watched Breena and Aislin gathering armfuls of firewood and dumping it on the grass, "What's so sacrilegious about playing pretend and dress up in the woods?"

If Vivien were meaner, she would've called him out on the topic change, but Vivien never liked being mean. But she liked poking and prodding, testing how far he would let her go before he stopped her. But this was his documentary after all and who was she to stop the show, "Normal kid stuff was sacrilegious in Devil's Pointe. Besides, that was just when we were kids. By the time we were teens we had upgraded to reading each other Romantic poetry and throwing little parties for ourselves. We were all in this Greek tragedy phase and liked to imagine that we were the Bacchae. We didn't really care if anyone saw us, but I'm sure you can picture how well people reacted to that—our families in particular."

Vivien supposed, out of all the girls, she had it the easiest. The only time her mother was ever lucid for longer than a few hours was on Sunday for the church service. It was the only day her mother would be awake, angry, looking for a reason to lock Vivien in the closet of mirrors while screaming at her through the door. It was the only day Vivien's mother spoke to her, reminding her of her father's death. Blamed her for it. It wasn't like Vivien was undeserving of the anger, the hatred, the punishment. Her mother had never forgiven her for what happened on her tenth birthday.

But Vivien could handle her mother's wrath once a week. The rest of the girls had their families lording over them with the hand of God every single day: Aislin's stepmother and sisters, Breena's grandmother, and Poppy's parents. It was why Vivien's home was so often their only reprieve from the outside world besides the woods.

"You wrote a lot of poetry about that, the Bacchae. What drew you to them?"

Vivien sighed airily, "We liked anything about unhinged girls wreaking havoc in society. It seemed fitting to model ourselves after the way the rest of the world saw us."

"How did you all see each other?"

"We were just kids, little girls that wanted to fit in with the other kids at school and go to birthday parties and sleepovers. It wasn't our fault that we didn't fit in with anyone but each other."

Jamie was silent for a moment, eyes taking her in. She saw the way his eyes hungrily raked over Aislin whenever she walked past him, seen the flare of annoyance that crossed his face whenever he and Breena came into contact. But he didn't look at Vivien like that. He kept his face as stoic and composed as a statue, but underneath the stone was fear. She could smell it coming off him in delicious, delirious waves that made her stomach groan.

He was a deer—rigid and oh so still—waiting for the predator hiding in the forest to leap out and devour him.

"Was it the same way at the Farm?"

"Even worse. All the girls there either hated us or pretended we didn't exist. Bethany and her friends never liked us after the spring formal incident, but her rage only increased once we joined her at the Farm. *You're poisonous leeches.* That's what she called us. Poisonous leeches." Vivien chuckled to herself.

If their parents were the gods of their households, Bethany was the god of the Farm. Striking at the girls whenever they stepped even a toe out of line. She blamed them for every little thing that went wrong or wasn't done properly.

The cafeteria tables weren't clean? Poppy must have ditched her chores.

The garden supplies were misplaced? Vivien must have hidden them.

The office windows were left open? Breena must have broken in.

The gate to one of the animal stalls broke? Aislin must have let them out.

"I can't really blame her. We weren't very welcoming either. I didn't care about anyone besides Poppy, Aislin, and Breena. The rest of them were only following what their parents told them—to stay as far away from us as they could—and besides, isn't that what we all do anyways? Blindly listen to whatever our parents have to say, even if it hurts us?"

"That's a very forgiving stance."

"With parents like ours, you learn to be as forgiving as Saint Maria."

"Breena said that's why you all got along so well, because your families were all *psychotic.*" Jamie used air quotes to mirror

Breena's speech.

Vivien nodded, "She's right, though her wording is a bit more scathing than I'd like. Our families were all plagued by the same unrelenting feeling that we weren't who we were supposed to be. The Freels convinced our parents that we were all demon snatched or demonically possessed. They tried all kinds of rituals to exorcise us—starvation, tying us to beds, praying over us throughout the night, never letting us sleep—but nothing they ever did was as bad as sending us to the Farm."

"What was it like on the Farm that made it so bad? I'd think nothing could be worse than being exorcised."

"On the outside, the Farm looked like a reputable rehabilitation camp for troublesome girls. There was a rec room and sports supplies, a fancy cafeteria, lake activities. But none of that was for actual use. It was all for show. For us, they had educational videos that they made us watch over and over again in the dead of night. Everyone was given the same white dress to wear every day, sneakers, and winter gear for the colder months. Meals were only given to us if we managed to go a full two weeks without misbehaving, otherwise we were left with granola bars and water. The chores weren't all that bad, just your standard cleaning and care of the animals. But the punishments—" Vivien's throat tightened.

Jamie leaned forward, resting his elbows on his knees. The fear in his eyes had been replaced with fascination. He liked making her squirm, liked digging his nails into her wounds just so he could watch her bleed. But two could play at that game.

"What were the punishments like?"

She wanted to turn back to the stove and keep stirring the soup to give her hands something to do, to give herself something to focus on. But she wouldn't give him the satisfaction.

If Poppy taught her anything, it was that she wasn't the little lamb lost in the woods anymore, "One time, I tripped over the mop bucket while cleaning Pastor Freel's office and some of the water got onto these documents he had left out and completely ruined them. When he found out, he made me stand in the rain the entire night. I wasn't allowed to sit down or move or fall asleep. He had these cameras set up around the camp so he could watch us whenever he wanted to. The next morning, I was shaking so hard I couldn't stay still, no matter how warm my clothes were or how close I sat to the bonfire, and every time my teeth chattered too loudly, or I shook too hard, I'd get my hands whipped. I went to bed that night with my knuckles completely torn up. Poppy was the one that snuck into my cabin and put something on them to staunch the bleeding. She knew how to get around the Freel's surveillance."

"That sounds horrible."

Vivien shrugged and turned back to the soup, "At least when we were home, we got breaks. We could sneak out and get away from it all. But the supervisors at the Farm made sure that Aislin, Breena, Poppy, and I were separated at all times. We couldn't even look at one another without getting screamed at, locked in the storm cellar, or beat. Poppy was the pastor's prized daughter, and the rest of us were the heathens that led her astray. I think that's why it was so awful for us."

"All in an effort to fix you?"

"They didn't want to fix us, they wanted to break us. To them, we were nothing more than rabid animals biting at their ankles. Everything we did, no matter how perfect or pristine, became an insult. Better to not try at all than keep messing up. That's what they wanted to drill into us."

"I'm guessing that didn't work." He said it like a statement.

Like he already knew exactly what she was going to say and how.

Vivien laughed, "Of course not. It only made us worse. If we were going to get in trouble regardless, we figured we may as well do something to deserve it."

"Like what?"

"We ran off. We all snuck out of our cabins a few months after we arrived, and we just ran. Our plan was to get to the road and flag someone down to drive us out of the mountains, out of the state. Even if they caught us, it would've been worth it to at least try. Anything would have been better than Devil's Pointe."

Outside, Breena and Aislin were building the bonfire. Though it had rained recently, Pastor Freel always kept a shed full of dry wood, so the girls didn't have to worry about the weather. The clouds vanished, leaving a clear sky the color of burnished gold.

"We thought we would find the road. We thought getting caught by Pastor Freel or one of the supervisors was the worst thing that could happen, but it wasn't."

It would be dark soon; the bonfire would be lit and then it would be time to eat.

Vivien - Middle School

Vivien didn't remember much before her tenth birthday. It was the first time she felt like a human. The first time she really noticed things. The first time she made sure to look and observe and catalog everything around her.

For her birthday, Vivien adorned herself in a lavender dress with white lace trim and a white collar. She put on her softest socks and her best church shoes, braided her hair, and even snuck a tube of light-colored lipstick from her mother's vanity. It was subtle enough that no one would be able to tell that she was wearing it. But she could see it and that alone was enough to make a small blush creep up her cheeks in secret excitement.

And besides, it wasn't like either of her parents ever looked at her. They had an odd tendency to stare at the space just above her head, or right over her shoulder whenever they wanted to pretend to look at her. They did that a lot—pretend. Pretend to look at her, pretend to speak to her, pretend she didn't exist. Sometimes she wanted to grab them by the shoulders and shake them, to scream at them to look at her, to see her. But that would only get her locked in the closet with all of the mirrors and she didn't like the mirrors. So, she went along with their games of pretend, moved through the house like a winter breeze, invisible but felt.

Her mother had fallen asleep upstairs an hour before the party started. Vivien had seen her taking a few pills in the bathroom before washing them down with a glass of amber liquid. She did that a lot. It didn't start happening until after Vivien was born. The counselor said her mother had postpartum depression, though Vivien hadn't known what that meant or why exactly that explanation didn't exactly sit right with her. There was something more. Something else.

Or maybe Vivien just didn't like the counselor. She had started seeing him after the court mandated it when her mother had driven the both of them directly into oncoming traffic the year prior. She had been taking the pills then too.

None of her birthday balloons floated. Unless she kicked them or tossed them, they stayed on the ground. She had blown them up herself and she spent most of the morning trying to teach them to fly but to no avail, so she distracted herself by eating the store-bought birthday cake that was on the counter. She spent weeks saving money that she found between the couch cushions, on the ground outside, in the washing machine. It was all white and completely blank except for a small balloon frosted in the corner. Vivien had done that herself and she was quite proud of it.

She supposed other kids might have made fun of her for that, but it didn't matter because she didn't have many friends, if any at all.

Her father spent most of the morning mumbling to the invisible man in the corner of the backyard behind the apple tree. He did that a lot too. Sometimes, he would spend hours just standing outside in the rain or under the sweltering sun talking to the empty air. She didn't know when that started or why. The counselor didn't often talk about her father, which was fine because Vivien didn't often like talking about him. He rarely, if ever, spoke to her. He grunted and sighed and walked through the house like a ghost. So Vivien treated him like one.

She thought that was what he wanted. She thought it made him happy. Sometimes she thought she saw a small smile grace his lips when they sat together in complete silence and ate dinner without looking at one another. But on her tenth birthday, Vivien discovered there were many things she was wrong about.

She thought that the large knife in her father's hand had been meant for cutting the cake.

She thought that the odd mumbling coming from his mouth was his version of the happy birthday song.

You stole her. Bring her back. Where did she go? What did you do to her? I have to do this.

The words didn't make sense to her, but there were so many different birthday songs she heard on TV that she didn't think too hard about it. She was too distracted with the way her heart leapt in her chest at the sight of her father coming to her, talking to her, looking at her.

She thought that her father was grabbing her shoulders so he could hug her and celebrate her birthday with her.

"I have to do this. *He* needs me to. I need to get my Vivien back. You'll come back, won't you?" He brushed his hand over her the top of her head in a caress so soft tears slipped down Vivien's cheeks and splattered on the counter.

How long had she prayed for this? How many times had she dreamt of this? How often had she imagined the way her parents would hold her to their chests, run their fingers through her hair, kiss the top of her head.

It wasn't until her father dug the knife into her stomach that she realized that she was very, very wrong.

Her birthday hat fell off her head and the elastic dug into the skin of her neck, tricking her into thinking she couldn't breathe. Vivien's throat burned from the screaming and the tears, but her father's large, large hand covered her mouth, so no sounds came out. His hand was so big it could have covered her entire face.

Her stomach hurt and she felt sticky, but not from the frosting that had gotten all over her hands earlier that morning. That same stickiness was leaking out of the corner of her mouth like fruit juice, but it didn't taste like fruit juice.

He looked at her with dark, dark, dark eyes in a way she had never seen before. It was the first time he ever really looked at her. For a moment, she thought she could see a flash of something sad in his face and she couldn't stop herself from resting a hand on his cheek to soothe it away. She didn't want him to be sad. Didn't want the first time he saw her to be filled with anguish.

The feeling of her father grabbing her arms in his brought her attention back to kitchen. She fell on the floor and the white tile was so cold it seeped into her dress. Her father hovered over her, knees on either side of her body. He pulled the knife from her stomach and started hacking off her hands. She didn't know why he chose her hands to mutilate, but she supposed not everyone had a reason for doing what they do.

Where was her mother? Why couldn't she hear her? Could anyone hear her?

When he was done, he got up and left her in the middle of the kitchen.

That was her first solid memory.

The second was when she killed her father.

She didn't mean to. She was just so upset. Angry. Betrayed. Confused, so confused.

Somehow, she healed. Or maybe she imagined her father cutting off her hands. Either way, she still had her hands. She didn't know how long she laid there, but when she got up the afternoon sun had fallen out of the sky, washing the house in shadows. The knife lay on the floor in a puddle of her blood—a few feet away lay her hands, bloodied disembodied stumps, though she still didn't know if they had been real. If she were smarter, she would have left the knife, but her fear overrode any rational thought, so she grabbed it in her tiny hands, needing two to be able to carry it.

She found her father praying on the floor of their living room. In front of him, was a family portrait hanging over the fireplace. Her mother: youthful, smiling face surrounded by a halo of dark curls. Her father: bright and stoic, though the sparkle in his eyes gave away his happiness. Vivien: a baby, swaddled in a light purple blanket covered in lambs. It was the only picture in their house of all of them together. It was the only picture of any of them in their home.

Her father laid his head against the cold wood floor begging God to forgive him. Tears hit the floor beneath him in a soft drip, drip, drip.

I had to. She isn't her. She stole her. It's her fault.

Who was he talking about? He thought Vivien had done something to someone though she had no idea who or what. She couldn't steal a person. She never once stole something from a store or her parents, except that tube of lipstick from this morning.

Was that what this was about? She was going to put it back.

Was she bad now? Was she not good anymore?

Blame is a very heavy burden for a child to bear, so she curled it up into a little ball and held it close to her chest. She tried to be good. She always tried to be good. She spent hours praying at the foot of her bed every night for a smile, a hand on her shoulder, a kiss on her forehead. She'd clean and get good grades and read her Bible waiting for the day her parents would look at her and tell her how happy she made them. But that wasn't the lot in life Vivien had drawn. So she had to make do with what she had been given.

Her stomach and wrists still hurt and though her hands were fine, she could still feel the warm liquid trickling down the front of her soft dress—staining her white socks. Vivien stared at those white, now red, socks on her small, small feet and made the startling realization that if God forgave her father, he wasn't a very good God at all.

She stabbed him in the neck before he could scream, and she stood over his body as he bled out. It took him a while to stop twitching and gurgling. Blood bubbled up out of his mouth and splattered onto the floor, making her stomach churn and her head swim. She didn't really understand what was happening and she wouldn't understand for a long while, but it made her feel lighter knowing that he was hurting the same way she had been hurting.

"I'm sorry, Papa." Vivien had whispered, and when his eyes met hers, she stilled. His bright green eyes looked up at her and softened with a kind of reverence she hadn't known he was capable of. He reached out a hand and rested it on her arm, gentle as a feather and smearing his blood across her skin. If she looked hard enough, she could see something akin to forgiveness.

The smell of the blood did something to her, snapped

something into place, and she couldn't help herself. It was everywhere: soaking through to her underclothes, covering her arms and her scabbed kneecaps. She couldn't stop herself from lifting her little fingers to her face and licking the blood off of her hands and she couldn't stop herself from licking the blood off her father's fingers. Couldn't stop herself from sinking her teeth into his skin, as she held her father's hand the way she imagined Jesus held the apostles' feet as he washed them.

She thought that if she could consume him, she could keep a part of him with her forever. He'd never leave her. Never hurt her.

Her mother didn't come back downstairs until after Vivien chewed off her dad's finger. She looked at her daughter's bloodstained dress, the hole in the fabric right over her stomach, the finger in her mouth. It was also the first time, in a very long time, that Vivien's mother really looked at her. But instead of the love and adoration Vivien longed to see in her eyes, she was met with nothing but fear. This time, she didn't try to soothe it away.

Vivien caught a glimpse of herself in the reflection of the glass cabinet her mother kept her ceramic figurines in and fainted.

She woke up in the hospital a week later and didn't sleep again for the rest of her stay. From the whispered conversations between nurses, Vivien gathered that her father had tried to kill her, and he killed himself out of guilt. No one suspected Vivien of the act. How could they? She was so small, so young.

Vivien's mother said it was all a nightmare. But she knew better. Her father's blood on her hands and his finger in her mouth had been too real for her to dismiss as a dream.

She never asked what happened to her hands. Her mother

never told her.

As soon as she was discharged, Vivien and her mother moved to Devil's Pointe. Her mother had grown up there and they had all lived there when Vivien was a baby before they moved to the city. She was born a sickly little thing and they wanted to be closer to the hospital for all the appointments and tests and procedures.

Vivien had been born wrong. That's what her father had said. She had overheard them once while they sat together in the living room, and she had waited with bated breath for her mother to tell him that he was wrong. But the admonishment never came. She supposed now that her father had been right. Normal girls didn't hurt their parents. Normal girls didn't eat fingers or grow hungry at the sight of blood.

Sometimes she'd hear her parents mumble about her in their sleep as she stood over their beds, watching them.

For as long as she could remember, Vivien lived with the slithering, sickly feeling that they were going to disappear. That one day she would wake up and their house would be completely empty, save for her and her favorite stuffed animal Lamby. That feeling stayed with her as they buried her father, packed up the house, and left.

But if Vivien wasn't a normal girl, why should she try to pretend to be?

She wasn't quite sure what to make of Devil's Pointe when they arrived. The nights were eerily quiet, so quiet she could hear the spiders outside her window spinning their webs, and the days were spent languishing about her bedroom, bandaged and drugged.

The church services her mother dragged her to were always a somber and depressing affair, which Vivien enjoyed, but the people were too cheery and judgmental, which Vivien loathed.

She liked the library though. It was small and despite being right in the center of town, rarely anyone was ever in there. She'd hide between the shadows of the stacks and slip into any book she could get her hands on. She liked fairy tales and poetry because of the windy way the words would unfold.

She also liked Aislin. Hers was the only face Vivien didn't immediately want to gouge. She'd watch her in church, always sat between her two…sisters? Stepsisters? Vivien hadn't known which yet, but she hated them all the same. They'd pinch Aislin and whisper things in her ears that made her eyes lower to the ground. Her hair was choppy, and her clothes were a few sizes too big, shoes a size too small.

And though she always wore sleeves or dresses or pants that completely covered her, sometimes Vivien would see a bruise painting her wrist or a drop of blood staining a hem. She was hurting, plain as day, and yet no one ever acknowledged it.

If she knew how to make friends, Vivien would have tried talking to her while they stood behind one another waiting for communion, but she didn't know what to say or how to get her attention. Vivien wasn't used to existing next to niceties. She understood anger and the way her mother would pretend to not notice her at the dining room table.

Aislin's round, dark eyes were so sad and lonely that Vivien wanted nothing more than to rip her away from whatever family was taking care of her and run away into the woods with her. They could be like Peter Pan and Wendy or Huckleberry Finn and Tom Sawyer.

Vivien would braid flowers into Aislin's mousy brown hair, while Aislin would gather berries and nuts for them to eat.

They never spoke, but Vivien always found herself imagining

their shared lives together with a fondness that only came from knowing another's soul. She could tell that they were similar—in mind, body, or spirit she didn't know—and there was something in Aislin, a spark, a shadow, that mirrored Vivien's.

That same shadow was also in Poppy. But it wasn't just in her. It hovered over her small frame wherever she went and trailed after her like a blood hound.

While Aislin, and even that Breena girl from just outside of town, seemed to cower before that darkness that slipped out of them like that day in church or the party in the woods, Poppy embraced it like an avenging angel. She whispered words and commands to Aislin's stepsisters, the girls in the town square that would snicker at Breena as she walked by with her grandmother, the boys that would whistle and jeer at Vivien as she walked around the gas station with her slushie.

Vivien would watch as every single one of them would end up humiliated, crying, bleeding when Poppy was done with them.

Poppy had a rage that matched Vivien's and she wanted to know how to let it out. How to scream and rage and fight; and Poppy taught her just how to do that only a few months after Vivien moved to town.

When she wasn't spending her nights locked in the closet of mirrors, Vivien was sneaking out of the house once her mother put herself to bed with her pills and drinks.

Vivien liked the moonlight and the stars and the vast forest that looked like it would swallow her whole if she stepped onto the wrong path. She hated being in her bed, hated sleeping. Every night she was plagued with nightmares of her father. She'd dream of him coming back for her, of him finishing what he had started on her birthday. Only she didn't get up. She'd dream of that kitchen tile. Of the blood. Of her hands. The first and last time her parents looked her in the eye.

Anything was better than remembering her birthday.

One night, when Vivien was thirteen, while strolling between the dark trees, so tall she couldn't see where they ended and the sky began, she found Poppy hunched over a dead animal. The leaves had only just started changing and the way they would crunch under her boots echoed through the forest around her, drowning out any other noise.

A new school year started which meant new ways the other kids in her classes would torment her. Gum in her hair, crude drawings taped to her locker, getting shoved in the hallways, having books and class notes stolen from her backpack when she wasn't looking. That day had been particularly rough. Bethany had knocked her books to the floor and stomped all over her library copy of *Wuthering Heights* with her muddy loafers. She'd have to pay for the book now and the librarian would scold her. She hated being yelled at. Hated disappointing anyone.

She was so busy thinking about the next book from the library she wanted to read that she didn't noticed Poppy or the animal until she heard a small gasp come from just a few feet in front of her. The animal had been mauled so violently that Vivien couldn't figure out what exactly it even was. She could see that it was big, bigger than either her or Poppy. If it wasn't so dark, she thought she might be able to see its color, but from the way its fur sparkled in the moonlight, she guessed there was too much blood for her to see anyways.

At first, she thought she might have been dreaming. That the pink innards of the animal and the way it still gurgled and shuddered were just figments of her imagination, that she would wake up in her bed to discover that she hadn't snuck out of the house at all.

But there was no mistaking the smell of rot that lingered in the air or the way Poppy's sighs of relief made something coil in Vivien's stomach; ready to strike. The same something Vivien felt, she realized, when she watched her father grasping at the knife she had shoved into his neck.

"What are you doing out here all alone?" Poppy asked.

Vivien jumped back, startled out of her own head at the sound of Poppy's voice. Unable to find the words, she simply shrugged.

What was Poppy doing out here all alone? Did she go on walks at night too? Did she have trouble sleeping like me?

Poppy stood up and wiped the blood off her chin with the back of her hand, but she stayed standing over the animal, as if she were trying to shield it or protect it. If Vivien let her eyes blur over, Poppy would look like an angel—the tree branches behind her like giant wings.

"Don't worry, I found it like this. I wasn't the one that hurt it."

Vivien let out a startled laugh, more akin to a shriek, that echoed in the empty air between them, "Then what are you doing to it?"

Poppy gave her a knowing look that Vivien didn't quite understand yet, "I'm doing what we have to. You've felt it before. The hunger. You're feeling it right now. I bet you always feel it, right?"

Vivien nodded her head, eyes wide and fixed on the animal lying at Poppy's feet. It was still gurgling, exhaling uneven breaths that shuddered through its body, "How do you make it go away?"

The emptiness of her stomach seemed to grow so wide that she felt like it might cave in on itself. Her mouth twisted in envy as she watched the blood dripping from Poppy's mouth. Her hunger felt so vast that no matter how much she ate, it never seemed to go away.

"You can't. You just have to satiate it." Poppy reached out a hand towards Vivien as if she were trying to call over a rabid animal rather than a young girl.

Vivien took in the slight shake of Poppy's hand, the look of apprehension in her eyes. Poppy was nervous. She never imagined that Poppy could be nervous. She always walked through the town like she owned it, head held high and shoulders straight.

Without pause, Vivien stepped towards her and grabbed her hand. It was so soft, and Vivien sighed in relief when their hands met. She hadn't been held by another person for so long, ever maybe. She supposed she should have been scared, terrified even. Girls weren't supposed to be out in the woods this late at night. Girls weren't supposed to eat dead animals either. Or their fathers. But none of that seemed to matter anymore. She didn't care about what girls were supposed to do.

Poppy just held her hand, dipped their fingers in the blood, and brought them to Vivien's s mouth. She fed her like a newborn babe and held her while she cried. She wasn't sad. She was relieved. The ache that had been building inside of her finally settled. Eventually, the animal stopped moving and they left what was left of it when the sun started to rise.

"Aislin and Breena are like us too. They just don't know it yet," Poppy said as they strolled back towards town. The rising sun filtered through the trees, flickering little bits of sunlight across Poppy's face.

"Like us?"

Poppy shrugged and looked back at the woods they were leaving, "We're different. Everyone around us thinks we're wrong or bad for feeling the way we do, but we can't help it. It's just how we are. We aren't like regular people."

"Why not?"

"Because we aren't what we think we are. You know, there are these stories about babies that would get stolen from their cribs only to be replaced with something else. I think that's what happened to us."

Usually, Vivien rarely spoke. In her home of silence and empty glances, she could go days without talking to anyone except Lamby. But with Poppy, Vivien couldn't stop herself from talking, "My parents think I'm *wrong*. After my dad tried to hurt me, he said something like that. As if the *real* Vivien had been taken and I had stolen her place. I didn't understand what he meant at the time, but now I'm starting to think he was right. I found this box with my birth date carved into its top under the floorboards of my mom's bedroom; there was a lock of light brown hair, some little toys, and a baby picture of me. Or I thought it was me. Sometimes, I'd watch her as she pulled it out and cry over it. She'd hold my baby blanket to her chest and just sob. She never noticed me, but I always noticed her."

Poppy's hand gripped her tighter and she smiled at her, a soft but dazzling smile, "My parents think I'm a demon. That I was sent by the devil to test their faith. They just haven't figured out how to get rid of me yet."

"I don't think you're a demon."

"I don't think you're wrong."

When the trees broke, and the girls were left standing in the open air, they walked back to Vivien's home, washed up, and changed clothes. Later, Poppy dragged her into town where they found Aislin sitting at the fountain, and Breena waiting in line at the pharmacy while her grandmother grabbed milk from the refrigerator aisle.

Together, the four of them snuck into the back of the church and ate communion wafers, sat shoulder to shoulder, arm to arm in a little corner.

They found a few pairs of beaten up roller-skates in the church attic and spent the rest of the day skating around town, laughing and holding hands and whispering secrets to the wind.

"We finally found each other," Poppy whispered to them as they sat around the town sign welcoming anyone unlucky enough to come across Devil's Pointe.

Vivien - Present

The soup simmered on the stove as Vivien went about setting the table. Jamie stayed seated by the bay window, watching her like a hunting dog. Breena and Aislin had long since finished building the bonfire, but the pair stayed outside, just out of view, so Vivien and Jamie could keep talking.

"What happened after you all ran away from the Farm?"

"Didn't you do your research? We don't remember." Vivien smirked to herself, and she began rifling through the cabinets in search of wine glasses.

The last time the three of them had been up to the cabin, they had broken most, if not all of the wine glasses. So, before they left, they had made a trip into the nearest town to buy a new set. Aislin had been the one to put them away, but, like Poppy, she liked chaos and had a knack for hiding things in the most obvious places, which always made them far harder to find.

"You told the police that you didn't remember when they first found you. Memories have a tendency to sneak up on you with time." Jamie shrugged.

Vivien ignored him and continued gathering the dishes. "Let's eat first," she said, "then I'll tell you what happened."

Jamie nodded in agreement and shut his camera off, before

setting it down in the living room.

Vivien brought the soup over to the table and ladled it into the four bowls. The room filled with the scent of beef broth and mushrooms and if Vivien closed her eyes, she could pretend it was Poppy standing in the entryway of the kitchen and not Jamie. She could pretend it was Poppy's soft breathing and steady heartbeat that met her ears, not Jamie's.

Breena was right, Jamie was ruining their time in the cabin. But it was needed. The girls needed someone to test them, push them.

She left the soup on the table and made her way to the back of the cabin where Aislin and Breena were sitting on the garden bench beside the back door. For a moment, her heart stuttered in her chest, battering against it like a wasp stuck in a jar, when she saw the garden empty.

It never got easier, coming to the cabin without Poppy. Vivien kept waiting for the day she would walk outside to find Poppy tending to her mother's garden or standing at the tree line and watching the crows flit from tree to tree.

Sometimes, Vivien would catch a flash of dark auburn hair while walking down the street or hear the same lilting laugh that she was all too familiar with, and she'd stop dead in her tracks in a desperate attempt to find her. But it was never her. Never Poppy.

The night before she drove up to the cabin, she had a dream that she was buried alive. She was trapped in a wooden coffin, barely large enough for her to move, and she could feel the worms and beetles squirming over her. The more she tried to bang on or claw at the wood, the more dirt and bugs fell on her face, into her mouth. She could hear Poppy's voice, just above her, calling to her, but Poppy couldn't help her.

She had woken up covered in sweat, her clothes and the sheets sticking to her bare legs and arms. Sleep had evaded her for the rest of the night, just like every other night she had that nightmare.

Even in her dreams, she couldn't get to Poppy, and the reality was no different.

"The food's done," Vivien said, not bothering to mask the slight shake in her voice. Her eyes still lingered over the dense trees just beyond the edge of the garden, still searching for Poppy among the foliage. She could feel her in the breeze that tousled her dark hair. Could hear her voice in the shaking treetops. But she would give anything to see her again.

She startled at the feeling of a small hand, enclosing her wrist. When she turned, she half-expected Poppy's large eyes to be staring back at her. But it was Aislin that grabbed her.

"She isn't there, Vivien." Her soft voice fluttered around them, as she brushed Vivien's hair away from her face. "But it won't be long now." There was a hunger in her eyes and a small smile on her face that settled Vivien.

Vivien nodded her head and led the two other girls back inside.

Once the girls grabbed their bowls, they walked outside. Jamie followed their trio to the bonfire and watched as they set it aflame. Vivien told him to bring his camera so they could continue their interview. There was only one story left—the only story he actually cared about—and she wanted to tell him before it was too late.

Vivien settled onto one of the blankets that Aislin and Breena had set out, slowly eating her soup. The heat from the fire danced along her skin and set shivers racing up her arms. Jamie sat beside her, while Aislin and Breena sat only a short distance away.

"Are you sure you want to tell the story now? We can wait until we're finished eating." Jamie offered.

Vivien merely shook her head, "It's ok. It feels right to tell you the story like this."

Jamie finished setting up his camera, and she watched him with careful eyes as he ate his soup. "So, what was the last straw? What finally convinced you all to leave the Farm?"

"Poppy got locked in the storm cellar. I don't remember what for, Poppy's misbehavior was always much more muddled compared to us. But after the seventh day without her, the three of us snuck off to see where she was. At that point, we had figured out how to skirt around the security cameras. We waited for Pastor Freel and the priest to leave, and we snuck in once we knew they weren't coming back. They had Poppy chained to this old, tattered mattress on the ground. She was barely awake, slurring all her words. Her lips were chapped, and her skin was practically white. She had sweat through her clothes and was shivering so hard I was scared she was going to break her teeth."

"What were they doing to her?"

Vivien forced down a shudder, "They were performing an exorcism. The Freels thought Poppy had been possessed. It had been happening for a while, and we all knew it, but we had never seen it." They weren't like the other girls. They couldn't be fixed, reformed, molded into the perfect daughters. They'd kill them before that happened, either by accident or on purpose.

"She was so thin we were able to slip her hands through the ropes binding her. When we ran from the camp, we thought we would be able to find our way through the forest. We knew what way we had to go—had charted the path to our freedom weeks in advance. We were prepared, even in the dark. A few days before, Poppy had tagged trees and left markers so we would know the exact path we needed to take. We knew exactly where to go and how to get there. But the faeries don't like to play fair. I'm sure you know that." She searched his eyes for surprise, shock, a flinch, but she was met with a stone wall.

"The fae can be quite harrowing if you get on their bad side," he said, as simply as if he were reading off a grocery list.

Poppy had always been a believer in the faeries. Had thought that they themselves were changelings; faerie children swapped for sickly human babies. Jamie might not have been like them, but Vivien knew that his sister had been. His movie was too on the nose. The lore was too accurate. She knew that he would understand, that the three of them wouldn't have to seduce him to get him on their side. To get him to understand.

"We got lost. Kept passing the same tree over and over and over again for hours, days maybe, until Breena puked. We lost track of how long we had been in that forest. Our arms were numb from carrying Poppy, and at some point, we were all just so tired that we had to stop and lie down. That was when we saw the tunnel. I thought we might've been hallucinating from hunger or dehydration. But it was real."

That night, the forest that had once enveloped them in warm arms had become a labyrinth they didn't know how to escape. The shadows had choked them, stolen the air from the lungs and left them dizzy. But when they stumbled upon the tunnel, nestled into the side of a small hill, the unease that had sunk its claws into their skin dissipated and everything just felt right. They were still starving and so drowsy the only way they could stand was by leaning against one another, but none of that mattered anymore.

"We didn't know what or why, but something in the tunnel called to us. There were echoes of music and laughter spilling out of it, and we could feel it singing through our bone marrow. So we followed it. Got on our hands and knees and climbed into the tunnel."

"What did you find inside of it?"

Vivien tried to speak about it, put its beauty into words but they got caught in her throat so hard she had to cough. "Do you remember when you were little and you'd have these wild and fantastical dreams, but the moment you woke up they would slip through your hands like sand on a beach? That's how I remember that night. Everything was so vivid and if I try, I can grasp at tangible images but the second I have them, they just—" Vivien took a deep breath, "slip away. I remember when we came out the other end of the tunnel, we were at a party of some kind, and Poppy—she was standing as tall and ethereal like always, even with the bruises and sunken eyes. It was like she was all better, like she had never been stuck in that cellar."

"The music was so loud we couldn't hear our own thoughts over the instruments and there were all these colors just floating around us. The people there grabbed our hands and lured us in. They fed us sickly sweet fruit and wine until we could barely walk straight. Everyone was dancing and laughing. We were dancing and laughing. We felt free and at peace. Everything fell into place and felt so right that we just knew Poppy was right about the fae. We always thought she was kidding when she told us we were changelings. At the time, the idea had been ridiculous, some half-cooked fantasy Poppy was still clinging to from our childhood. But she knew better. Poppy always knew better."

Jamie's breath grew labored, and his eyes were tinged with red.

He coughed once.

Twice.

"I remember seeing something, a fox or something, and the four of us just took off after it. We were still so hungry, and seeing it run away from us like that flooded our bodies with adrenaline. We chased it through the tunnels and back out into the forest. It was like instinct pushing us to hunt. I could hear its heartbeat and its panting. I could feel every step it took inside me. We cornered it in this meadow full of bluebells and it just stopped fighting us. It was so quiet, and I remember it just laid itself out in the middle of the flowers. Like it had chosen us to devour it, instead of the other way around. Poppy stood over us, telling us to eat. She told us that it was too late to save it and that we shouldn't let it go to waste."

Killing it would be merciful.

It'll always be a part of you.

Don't be sad, it's a dead thing anyways.

Poppy stood over the girls, her palms resting on their heads, fingers gliding through their hair, hands wiping the blood from their bodies. Vivien couldn't remember what animal they had eaten that night, but it hadn't tasted like anything they had ever had before. The blood was sweet and syrupy, the meat melted in their mouths, and all they could smell was Poppy's lilac perfume.

"What did you guys do?"

Vivien shrugged, her eyes never straying from the fire dancing before her, "We did what we were told. We drank the blood and bit into the meat like it was the first meal we had ever eaten. Poppy wanted us to eat it, so we did. She could have told us to walk into the middle of traffic and we would have listened. But she always had our best intentions at heart. She'd never hurt us. We would've died out there if she hadn't pushed us to eat. You have to understand that.

"Poppy cleaned us up when we were done, and she kissed each of our foreheads goodnight as we drifted off to sleep—stomachs full and bodies satiated. I could almost hear her talking to us while we slept. She sounded so sad, like she was saying goodbye. When we woke up, we were all laid out side by side under this tree, and there wasn't a speck of dirt or drop of blood on us. But Poppy was nowhere to be found.

"I could still taste the blood and skin in the back of my throat. Sometimes I still wonder what—or who—that animal was that we ate. I still wonder if we had done something to Poppy. But every time I try to think back to the night, there are all these shimmering lapses in my mind. Like the memories are there, but I'm seeing them underwater—muffled and distorted. The official police report says we were gone for three months, but it only felt like a few hours to us."

"Some hunting dog found us in the middle of the woods, and its owner called the police. The volunteer search parties had given up hope they'd find us alive a month after we vanished, so they didn't believe the guy at first. But once the cops arrived, there was no denying the fact that we were alive. We spent the rest of the day being interrogated at the hospital until the Freels came to pick us up and they finally let us go back home." *Home.* The word sat bitterly on her tongue, souring her spit.

Jamie looked up at the sky, and Vivien wondered how many stars he was seeing.

"I made a black out poem with the police reports." Vivien continued, "It was the only poem I made about that night. I didn't want to feel the way I felt when I first woke up tied to that tree, so I kept that night away from my art. We all did. But the poetry book felt incomplete without it. Messing with the police report seemed like the most clinical way I could face what happened to us. To her."

"How *did* that make you feel? When you woke up and thought you had killed your friend?" Jamie was slurring his words, and Vivien wondered how long it would take before the soup did what it needed to.

"It was one of the worst moments of my life. Second only to the moment I realized Poppy wasn't with us." Vivien had screamed when she woke up, nails clawing at the police officer who had tried to check her pulse. Her nails had been broken and bloody by the time the EMTs had gotten her onto a gurney. "Some conspiracy theorists thought that we had been *pixie-led*. That the faeries decided to mess with us, steal us away, confuse us. Hurt us."

"What do you think happened?"

"Some people believe that the souls of the dead would join the faeries in their realm. Maybe Poppy died and we saw her ghost haunting that party under the hill. All I know is that she was there with us in the forest, in that tunnel. I could feel her skin beneath my fingertips and smell the grass in her hair. She was real. We made a promise that we all would stay together. She couldn't just leave us, which is why we need to find her again."

Did we save her? Did we kill her?

Was there a difference?

The same questions that had plagued her all these years continued to swim through her mind.

Grief stained her like the juice from a pomegranate. It

chewed her up and spit her back out onto the sterile floor of the hospital room she had been put into. Poppy had curled her way into Vivien's veins and once she was gone, Vivien was left void of the warmth she had gotten used to. She waited for the haunting, for Poppy's ghost to come rasping on her window like Catherine Earnshaw, but there was nothing. Poppy vanished, and with her went all the magic they had found together.

There was no body to bury, no final memory to hold onto, no last words to comfort them.

She was just gone.

None of them could let her go.

"Maybe she would want you to let go—" Jamie dropped his bowl, the soup spilling over the front of his shirt and down his pants. He tried to speak, but Vivien only shushed him and helped lay him down, so he didn't hit his head when he fell over.

"We can't. We are, and forever will be, bound to one another. If one dies, the rest of us have to follow." She brushed his hair away from his face and pet his cheek, "It'll be ok. Just close your eyes and go to sleep. It'll be over soon."

Vivien gathered the bowls and walked inside, Aislin and Breena following close behind. They'd find Poppy again.

Sometime later, Jamie woke up. He groaned in pain, and Vivien watched as he used his shaking arms to sit himself upright. She could practically hear the rapid-fire thoughts and confusion that clouded his mind. His heart was racing and sweat dripped from his pores.

"I slipped something in the soup. It's not meant to kill you, just disorient you a bit."

He stared at her, eyes unfocused and wide as he took in her white dress and bare feet. It was the dress all the girls were given when they first arrived at the Farm. It was the dress she and the rest of the girls had been wearing when they went missing.

The same dress Aislin and Breena were also wearing.

"What's going on?" Jamie ran his hands through his hair and down his face.

In another world, Vivien might have felt sorry for him, but she couldn't let herself feel anything for him. Just like she couldn't let herself feel anything for the other boys that came before him. Every year they came up to the cabin in search of that tunnel, and every year they came up empty. They had never been able to find it again, to find Poppy.

That was why they needed Jamie. He forced their old wounds open and played in the blood that spilled out of them for the sake of his own art. They had needed to talk, to face every awful thing they had ever done and accept it. Poppy had never shied away from what she truly was. She embraced it and flourished once that burden had been lifted off her shoulders.

That had to be the real reason she didn't come back with them.

There was no world where Poppy didn't exist alongside them. There couldn't be. She was the air they breathed and the water they drank. She couldn't be gone. She wouldn't leave them behind like that.

Nothing mattered to Poppy more than her girls. Their love for each other was like a knife, twisting and stabbing at the open air in their direction before finally hitting its target. To love was to spill blood, to bathe in it. None of them knew how to love gently, softly. They loved with teeth and fists and knives. They loved with pain and bruises and cuts that ran so deep they couldn't be stitched back together. Every hug ended with broken ribs, every touch left scrapes littering their skin, and every kiss left purple and blue marks in their wake. But they never shied away from the pain. It was all they knew.

"It isn't anything against you. You were a means to an end. Besides," Vivien paused, watching him as he struggled to stand. "The soup was only the beginning. We haven't even gotten to the meat yet."

"The meat—" Jamie puked in the grass. Vivien brushed her fingers through his hair and laid a gentle hand on his shoulder.

Breena scrunched up her nose at him. This would be easy for her, enjoyable even. She hadn't liked him from the beginning. "You. You're the meat. It would be easier just to eat you now, but we do love a good chase." She couldn't stop the smile from spreading across her face.

Aislin and Breena were always so hesitant at the beginning. They didn't like the luring, the seduction. But they craved the violence, had gotten so used to the feeling of ripping into something that they needed it like air.

The first year had been the hardest, the sloppiest.

They had gone up to the cabin on a whim, desperate to cling to any shred of Poppy that they had left. Poppy's home had already been sold, and the rest of Devil's Pointe had been too tainted with bad memories and bad people for them to go back. The town bred the very judgment and hellfire that had sent them off to the Farm. If it hadn't been for them, if they hadn't been sent off to the Farm, Poppy would still be here with them, standing beside them.

It had been the last day of their trip when a lost hiker had stumbled across their cabin. The girls hadn't planned on hurting him. But they had been hungry, angry, broken. It was a pain raw meat couldn't satisfy. They needed the kill, needed to witness the pain of something outside of themselves. He had broken his arm, and there had been so much blood the girls couldn't see straight. It had felt like a blessing, an offering. They had just attacked, acted on instinct. It was only after they got their fill that the music started. In that moment, they were back under the hill, and though they tried following it, they couldn't find the tunnel.

It became a tradition for them to hunt. Every year, some poor, unsuspecting soul would happen upon the cabin, and they would never come back out of the woods. Every year they'd gorge themselves and every year they'd hear the music, only to follow it and find nothing. There was no hill, no tunnel, no Poppy.

When Jamie spent weeks writing her email after email, begging her to let him interview them, it had felt like another offering. The sacrificial lamb willingly orchestrated its own slaughter. It was pure coincidence that his sister had suffered a similar fate to Poppy. Vivien had read every article, every think piece, every Reddit thread, and they all led her to the same conclusion.

Vivien turned Jamie's face towards her own, "You understand, don't you? Your sister was like us, right? A changeling trapped in a body she didn't understand, couldn't control? It's an urge we have to satiate, an itch we need to scratch."

He shook his head, "You're nothing like her," Jamie said, trying his best to keep his voice clear.

Vivien's head was spinning, and the colors of the forest danced around her, like embers flying up to the sky from the pyre standing before them.

Jamie climbed to his knees, digging his hands into the dirt in search of some sensation that could ground him. Vivien had done the same thing. That day in the forest, before the EMTs had arrived on the scene, she sat kneeling in the ground and ripping up the grass beneath her fingertips. She had been so empty, she needed to be reminded that what was happening had been real. That it hadn't been another nightmare.

"All humans are capable of being monsters," Vivien said, digging her nails into his arm, "The difference is you try to hide it. Suppress it. But that only makes it worse. Every horrible thought you've ever had, every wretched action you've ever plotted sits inside your chest, stays simmering within you, until one day you can't control it. It all spills over and hurts the ones around you, and you have no one to blame but yourself. This is how we purge it, embrace it."

"We'll give you a head start," Aislin said, coming to stand beside Vivien. She had been the one to deal with the camera. Breena wanted to destroy it and his laptop, but Vivien had stopped her.

By the time anyone found the footage, they would all be long gone—if anyone found it at all. Who cared who saw it, what they thought. They could make their theories and guesses, but no one would know the full truth.

Vivien watched as Jamie's face elongated, she listened as his bones snapped and popped, tearing through his skin. She could almost taste the metal of his blood as it wept from his wounds. She watched his ears lengthen to points atop his head and his teeth sharpened. His skin stretched and molded over the wounds and bright orange fur dusted his body.

Jamie was the fox, and they were the hunters.

He stood on his shaking hind legs and took off into the woods. Breena howled in delight as she chased after him, Aislin and Vivien following after.

They bounded after him like wolves, like the hounds that chased Actaeon.

The trees blurred past them, and the wind whipped through their hair. Branches cut into their arms, and the foliage on the ground sliced the bottoms of their feet, but they barely felt the sting of pain. There was nothing but their thundering heartbeats and the scent of Jamie's fear. It was so palpable Vivien could taste it spilling over her tongue.

In some stories, the faerie maidens hid their hooved feet under their dresses, luring the men into their trap before devouring their hearts. Vivien imagined her own feet turning to hooves, protecting her soles from the harsh forest ground.

He had gotten farther than they expected but he didn't know the woods like they did. There were so many paths he could have taken. So many directions he could have gone. It would have been easy for him to find a road, a campsite, a cabin. But he didn't. They never did. They always ran to the trees. They always got lost, too turned around in their own panic.

It was like the forest was repaying them, tricking their prey the same way it had tricked them the day they lost Poppy. It was an atonement, a prayer, a cry for forgiveness.

The trio took turns leading the hunt, ebbing and flowing around one another like waves crashing against the shore. The buzz that had filled her veins the night they chased that animal out of the tunnel filled her once more. She ran faster, beating her feet against the ground as hard as she could. They couldn't lose that feeling.

If she closed her eyes, she could pretend she was flying.

Breena was the first to grab him. She took a hold of his hair and pulled him into her. Then Aislin and Vivien grabbed his arms. They were no longer the girls they had grown up as.

No longer Aislin, Breena, and Vivien.

They were the Bacchae. The sirens that lured the lost to their doom. The faeries that fed off human suffering.

Jamie had wanted to use them for his own gain.

"You'll be with your sister soon," Vivien whispered to him as she, Aislin, and Breena held him against the forest ground.

The wind whistled in the trees. The animals hid under the brush and in the shadows.

Their teeth grew and their nails sharpened as they tore open his chest and began to feast.

They held his heart in their hands—his blood in their mouths—and that black pit that sat inside them seemed to lessen.

When all was said and done, the girls lay in the grass beside Jamie, a tangle of limbs and organs and blood matted hair, as the moonlight filtered through the treetops. Music filled the air around them and burrowed its way into their chests. They could feel the ground thumping beneath them from the dancing. Poppy's lilting laughter floated to them on a soft breeze.

When they shook off the lethargy from their tired limbs, they would walk through the forest hand in hand, following the sound that only the faeries could create. They would find that tunnel and climb into it going further and further under the hill. They would find Poppy dancing in the center of the faeries, her long hair swishing around her. She would still be wearing that white dress. She would run to them, crush them to her chest, trail her nose through their hair and they would pretend nothing bad had ever happened to them.

They would be those girls playing in the woods, singing and dancing while the rest of the world rushed by them. Because nothing else would matter.

They would be together again.

138

If you enjoyed this novella, or have any critiques you would like to share, please leave a review on Goodreads or Storygraph!

Acknowledgments

This novella was a long labor of love. During my time at Dartmouth, I knew I wanted to write something weird and gross and lonely. After being surrounded by professors (and even some students) who heralded niche literary fiction and nonfiction memoirs to be the purest form of writing, I was gnashing my teeth against the bars of my enclosure by the time my Independent Study was finishing up. While my writing was able to stand and shine on its own during class, I spent a long time having to prove the merits of genre-fiction, like horror, to my peers.

The first people on my list I want to thank are my Thesis advisors: Nancy Canepa, Barbara Kreiger, and Rena J. Mosteirin. Without the help and guidance of these three wonderful women, my Thesis would have remained a half-formed mass of flesh and nonsense piling up in the corner of my old studio apartment. I want to extend my sincerest gratitude towards them and thank them profusely for reading every chapter of this story and answering my long-winded emails with thought-provoking advice. This novella would not exist (and I wouldn't have my degree) had you not took me under your wing.

I'd also like to thank my dearest friends Daisy, for making my cover and a plethora of fanart, Ryan, for listening to every long winded voice note shared at 3 a.m. questioning whether my dialogue sounded weird or what the ending of my story should actually be, Ella, for reading my story and gifting me with my very first hardbound copy of *What We Consume*, Maddie, for writing stories with me in our dorm room and pushing me to be proactive, and Saffron, for being the best hype-man a friend could ask for. You all are so cherished and without your love, my story would be uninspired and empty.

Sneak Peak: "Promises to Keep"

There was a ghost standing just inside the gate of the *Little Whispers Orphan Home*.

As Scarlette Avery sat in the backseat of the yellow cab, she watched the way its translucent fingers combed through its red red hair. Watched the way its dark dark blue dress billowed in the breeze. Watched the way the grass swayed around and behind its pale pale feet. They were bare, caked in mud and blood.

It wasn't an unusual occurrence for Scarlette to see a ghost— or this ghost — at Little Whispers. But still, she never imagined that she would ever again see that ghost in her waking hours. Never imagined that she would ever again return to the hallowed grounds of the orphanage she had once called home.

She thumbed at the notebook in her lap, flipping through the pages that were stuffed full of dozens of unanswered letters and messages that she could never bring herself to finish or send. She pulled out the most recent letter, though she didn't know when it had been sent, and poured over it for what felt like the millionth time since she found it sitting on her bed. Her green painted fingernails skimmed over the wild loops and swirls of her old friend's handwriting.

"Are ya adopting? Look a little young to be pickin' up a kid." The driver spoke up. He watched her through the rear view mirror, but Scarlette kept her gaze focused outside the window.

They sat idling, waiting for the wrought iron gate surrounding the orphanage's property to be opened. They had been waiting for so long that Scarlette could imagine the ire in Miss Amara's face when she saw the oil stain that was no doubt leaking from under the cab.

The groundskeeper lived in a small cottage just a short walk from the main manor, nestled in a small patch of dense forest to keep it hidden away from anyone coming up the long, winding driveway.

Had they been expecting Scarlette, the groundskeeper would have been stationed outside prepared to open the gate. But no one was expecting Scarlette for at least another month.

"Not adopting. I'm moving in as a caretaker," Scarlette said as she stuffed the notebook into the bag beside her.

For a moment, she contemplated getting out of the cab to ring the gate's bell for the third time since they'd arrived. But Scarlette preferred the safety and comfort of the worn leather seats beneath her and the lingering smell of cigarette smoke and coffee over facing the ghost that had been slowly drifting ever closer to the cab.

The driver let out a long whistle and chuckled, "Good luck moving into this haunted house. You wouldn't believe the stories I've heard."

"Moving back," Scarlette said, her voice so low she hardly heard the words slip from her own mouth.

"Excuse me?"

"Moving back. I lived here until I was 15." She kept searching the tree line for the groundskeeper, but not even a shift in the bare tree branches could be found.

The driver's eyes widened, "Then you know about the girls?"

Scarlette opened her mouth to say something, but no words

would come out. She nodded her head, and the cab stayed quiet. There was nothing but the rumbling of the engine and the faint static coming from the radio.

The girls — Daisy, Annika, Isabella, Penelope. There were probably more. More girls, more blood.

Penelope — *no, the ghost, not Penelope* — remained behind the gate, but she had paused her movements.

"Why on earth would you come back here?"

Though it was now a dreary, gray November, Scarlette had made the decision to return to Lakewood Falls back in the early spring.

April had been a peculiar month. The weather too sticky, the clouds too heavy. Maybe it had been the early morning fog that rolled into Tina's, her foster mother's, garden. Or the never fading scent of incoming rain that clung to the dirt road just beyond the new porch Aaron, her foster father, had just built.

It hadn't rained once that whole month.

She had kept waiting for that first drop, kept holding her breath in anticipation of the sky opening up before the flood.

But it hadn't come.

She had been antsy, and as she sat on her porch swing, listening to the squeaking back and forth of its hinges, she thought of Lakewood Falls and the *Little Whispers Orphan Home.* Thought of the two best friends she had left behind. Thought of the fog that rolled and swirled across the grounds in the early morning. Thought of the missing girls and the woods and the way it always seemed to rain when another one vanished.

As the tall, grass swayed in the light spring breeze, she had thought of the stories the older boys in the orphan home used to tell the younger kids in front of the fireplace after dinner.

If you stare into the trees for too long, they'll eat you.

That's what had happened to all the kids that never got adopted. They spent too long at *Little Whispers*, stared too long at the forests that separated them from the rest of the world and got swallowed whole.

Or at least that's what the kids had all told themselves.

When she was little, Scarlette would always avoid looking out the windows, and she'd stare squarely at her shoes whenever she was walking outside. Even glimpsing at the trees beyond the walls of the orphan home had made her feel like all the air had been taken out of her lungs.

And she kept thinking of those stories and waiting and watching and dreaming of the thing in the woods coming to swallow her whole. Then, the letter came.

Miss Amara had written her, all these years later. She had lost one of her teachers at the orphan home and needed a speedy replacement. She promised to cover any and all expenses that would arise, so long as Scarlette agreed to come to the home and work for the next year.

That airtight, breathless feeling in her chest had only gone away the moment she saw the peeling paint and rotting wood of the *Welcome to Lakewood Falls* sign just outside of the town's limits. She remembered sighing in relief as she stuck her head out the window and breathed in the air around her. The cab driver merely shook his head at her, not understanding why she would ever want to come to this dead-end town. But Scarlette had needed to.

If Scarlette paid more attention, she would notice the way the ghost's blue eyes were now gray and milky. She would notice the blue veins spider-webbing under her too pallid skin. But Scarlette had learned early on, when she was nothing more than a mousy, waifish child, to never look too long at a ghost.

She had made that mistake once, a long long time ago. And she would not make that mistake again.

A knock on the window startled her out of her reverie. Looking up, Scarlette saw a young man hovering over the cab door. He waved at her through the glass, a tight smile resting on his face.

She rolled the window down and leaned her head out the window. With the rain speckled glass out of the way, Scarlette was able to take in the light blonde hair and familiar hazel eyes, but she couldn't quite place him. He was a pastor, if his starchy clothes were anything to go by. Maybe he had been an altar boy when Scarlette was a child.

"Good day to you ma'am. I work under Pastor Silas here. Can I help you with something? We weren't expecting any visitors today."

"My apologies. Miss Amara isn't expecting me for a few more weeks. I'm to be one of the new caretakers."

The pastor's eyes widened in surprise and he flashed her a too wide, too white smile. "What a pleasure to meet you. Let me help you up to the main house."

He opened the door and offered his hand to help Scarlette step out of the backseat. She grabbed the side of the door instead, and hauled herself out onto the road. If he had been offended by her rejection, he hadn't shown it. All he did was shut the door behind her and walk to the trunk.

The pop of the trunk unlocking echoed through the still air, and within seconds her bags and suitcase were being placed on the ground and the trunk was once again closed.

He grabbed her suitcase, but before he could pick up her bag, Scarlette had already snatched it up in her hands. She was perfectly capable of managing her own luggage.

Penelope — *the ghost* — had slipped silently back into the treeline. There was no red hair, no dark blue dress, no blood stained feet.

Scarlette paid the cab driver and waved him off as the pastor finally opened the gate. A trail of dark, dark oil spilling onto the cement. She'd have to remember to tell someone about the spot before Miss Amara saw it.

"Sorry about all this. Our groundskeeper is out running errands in town. His sister is sick, so he's gone to get her some medicine. You must have been waiting for a while. I'm Evan Morselli." He extended his hand towards her. "I don't think I got your name."

Scarlette couldn't recall the name, but there was something about him that bothered her. *Something something something.*

"Scarlette. Scarlette Avery." She shook his hand and ignored the chill that ran down her spine at the touch of his skin against hers. She made a mental note to find some antibacterial soap once she was settled in her room.

"Arabella's Scarlette? You grew up here with her and Clarissa?" Evan pushed the gate closed, locking them inside the property.

At the sound of Arabella and Clarissa's names, Scarlette flinched, keeping her mouth in a tight closed line.

"With the way she talks about you, I had thought you were dead." Evan laughed and waited for her to say something, but when she remained silent he continued filling the silence with his talking, "Arabella is the sick one I mentioned earlier, so you won't be able to see her today. It's nothing too serious, just a slight fever. She'll be better with some rest and fluids."

Scarlette's brow scrunched in confusion; Arabella didn't have a brother. Unless he meant...

"When you said the groundskeeper was getting his sister, Arabella, medicine, did you mean Gabriel?"

Evan nodded, and Scarlette couldn't stop the confused mumble that left her mouth. He stared at her quizzically, but kept any comments to himself.

Scarlette hadn't known Gabriel had come back. He had never been mentioned in any of the letters she'd gotten.

Evan walked her up the rest of the driveway and helped her bring her bags inside. "Miss Amara is volunteering at the Lakewood Falls food kitchen with Pastor Silas and won't be back until late tonight. Do you know where you'll be sleeping?"

Scarlette nodded, taking in the grand staircase in the entry way. "My old room. I stayed here long enough that I got my own room in the stewardess corridor before I was adopted out. Miss Amara told me that it was still empty."

"Yes," Evan said, smiling that too wide smile that showed off his too white teeth, "We've been fortunate enough lately that few of the children stay here into their teen-hood."

"Being here when you're any older than fourteen can be quite lonely. It's nice that more kids are being adopted."

Evan nodded along, still smiling that ghastly smile, and started prattling on about the home's latest bout of advertising stunts. Scarlette paid little attention to the words coming out of his mouth.

The foyer of the home was exactly as it was when she left: tall, tall ceilings with tall, tall windows and a crystal chandelier hanging just beyond the doorway. The walls were still a brilliant jade green: meant to calm the mind and keep the children happy, tranquil. Scarlette hated the color green. Her mother, her birth mother, had also hated the color. Though her memories of her mother were scrambled and hazy, she did remember that.

Beneath her feet were the creaky, ever groaning dark wood floors that she remembered slipping and sliding across in her stockings whenever Miss Amara, or any of the other stewardesses, had their backs turned.

Down the corridor, she could hear the shuffling of papers and the distant chatter of children talking in the hallways between classes. If she closed her eyes, she could see herself sitting on the floor in front of her locker, nestled safely between Clarissa and Arabella. If she closed her eyes, she could almost hear Clarissa's tinkling laugh, could almost feel the swish of Arabella's hair against Scarlette's arm.

But *those* images and memories were too distant now. They'd silently slipped too far beneath the surface of the murky water of her memory for her to properly recall them anymore.

Grabbing her bags, Scarlette made her way up the stairs. Evan followed close behind.

Her eyes raked over the children's artwork that Miss Amara decorated the walls with. There were crayon depictions of violets from the meadow in the backyard, finger paintings of girls braiding each other's hair, colored sketches of rabbits running in the woods and foxes bounding after them. There were a few pictures that Scarlette didn't recognize, pictures from girls and boys that came to the home long after Scarlette had left.

On the fifteenth step, hanging at eye level, was a picture of three blue and gray moths. The rest of the page was blank save for a few tiny scattered trees that had been drawn in the background. In the corner was Clarissa's name scribbled in her swirling, twirling script, alongside Scarlette's and Arabella's.

"That's quite lovely. The stewardesses are always—"

Scarlette put up a hand to stop him, "I'm here to work. Not adopt a child. You can stop with the car salesman act. I won't be leaving any time soon. Now if you'll excuse me, I'd like to take a bath and get some rest."

Evan muttered an apology before scurrying back down the steps and heading down the long hallway, likely leaving to head to the chapel. Scarlette sent a silent prayer to the ceiling above her in thanks. She hated the chapel.

Ignoring the rest of the colorful, messy pictures on the wall, Scarlette made her way up the rest of the stairs.

The first floor housed the classrooms and libraries, while the second and third floors housed the boys and girls dorms respectively. While the second floor was of no consequence to Scarlette, the third floor was another beast entirely.

Her foot skipped over the last step, an instinct she had developed throughout her years of sneaking in and out of the home.

How strange, she thought, *for my body to remember what my mind had forgotten.*

She dropped her bags and danced her hands over the old, wooden banister and let its cool, smooth surface settle back into her skin. The lights were dimmer up here than they were downstairs; the windows were coated in a thick layer of dust and film, and Scarlette couldn't tell when the ever flickering light bulbs had been changed last.

To anyone else, the orphan home would appear to be a labyrinth of long, twisting, winding hallways full of locked doors and cobwebs and soft yellow light. But to Scarlette, she had mastered the labyrinth years ago, bested the Minotaur, and escaped with more than a few broken bones. Her old room, or more accurately her new, old room, was down the leftmost corridor, and her feet should have been taking her in that direction. Instead, they took her down the path directly in front of her.

When they were girls, Miss Amara had split them all up throughout the third floor. Their rooms had never been placed near one another, and they were never allowed to room together. By the time they were old enough to have their own rooms, Miss Amara had only gotten stricter in keeping them apart. They had been given earlier bed times than the other girls, and their rooms were no longer allowed to even be in the same corridor. The trio had been relegated to separate corridors as far apart as they could be.

That hadn't stopped them from sneaking out or sleeping in each other's rooms, of course.

So it was really no surprise when Scarlette's feet led her right to Arabella's door all the way at the end of her designated hallway.

Had she kept the same room too?

The lettered stickers she had used to spell out her name down the side of the door frame were gone, but some of the sticky residue was still left behind. Had she been the one to peel them all off?

Scarlette's fingers hovered over the now barren door. She traced them over the wood grain and the chip near the door knob that Clarissa had left from when the door got stuck and trapped Arabella inside.

"Gabriel?" A soft voice called from inside the room. The sound made her heart leap in her chest, like a frog smashing itself against the glass of its cage.

Scarlette held her breath.

"Gabriel, is that you?"

There was a ruffling of bed sheets and soft mumblings of complaint. She counted the light footfalls approaching the door: one, two, three, and bolted back down the hallway.

She rounded the corner where she picked up her bags and heard a lock unlatch, heard a door swing open. Scarlette imagined the way Arabella's dark hair would be a mess of tangles and waves half covering her face as she looked up and down the hall for her *brother*. Imagined the way her skin would be flushed with fever, eyes hazy with confusion.

Scarlette didn't wait to see if Arabella would follow her. She just picked up her bags and ran to her new, old room. The door was unlocked, thankfully. She couldn't imagine how difficult it would have been trying to unlock it with how badly her hands were shaking.

She expected to be uncomfortable. She expected the nostalgia. Expected the flashbacks and waves of barely there memories. But the guilt settling in the pit of her stomach was something unexpected.

Tossing her bags into the room, Scarlette slammed the door shut behind her and sunk to the floor. She brushed her hair out of her face and clamped her hands over her ears.

The room was still dark and the faint scent of lemon and pine drifted to her nose. The usual scent of damp and moss had been scrubbed away, making the room feel wholly alien and wrong.

Though all of her pictures and sketches had been taken down, the wallpaper she had chosen when she moved in was still the same. It was one of the few comforts Miss Amara allowed them, as long as they did the redecorating themselves, of course.

Scarlette stared at that wallpaper — watercolor bouquets of violets against a cream background — as she laid her head against the cold hardwood floor. They had all gotten matching wallpaper: violets for Scarlette, chrysanthemums for Clarissa, and tulips for Arabella. Though she couldn't fully remember why they chose those flowers or what they meant, she recalled a night full of wine, spent hazy and warm in their secret hideout while Clarissa rambled off facts from her Victorian book on bouquet making.

Her eyes traced over those violet patterns until the seemingly never ending opening and closing of the girl's dormitory doors stopped and the room was blanketed in shadow.

She stayed curled up on the floor like a cat until the faint rays of sunlight poured through her white lace curtains and Miss Amara knocked on her door.

* * *

To stay up to date with my next novel, sign up for my newsletter at sarayahdanielle.com or follow me on Twitter @sarayah-danielle.

About the Author

Sarayah Danielle is an American author, born in Illinois. She holds a BA in English Literature from UIUC and a MA from Dartmouth College. After concluding her studies, she packed up her two cats (Misty Day and Piper Halliwell) and moved to Boston where she continues to cultivate her love of writing about Celtic faeries, girlhood, and cannibalism.

You can find more of her work at https://digitalcommons.dartmouth.edu/ by searching Sarayah Villasenor.

You can connect with me on:
- https://sarayahdanielle.com
- https://x.com/sarayahdanielle